To Die For

A MITCH COOPER Mystery

To Die For
A MITCH COOPER Mystery

BILL CRAIG

ABSOLUTELY AMAZING eBOOKS

ABSOLUTELY AMAZING eBOOKS

Published by Whiz Bang LLC, 926 Truman Avenue, Key West, Florida 33040, USA.

For information contact:
Publisher@AbsolutelyAmazingEbooks.com

ISBN-13: 978-1945772412 (Absolutely Amazing Ebooks)
ISBN-10: 1945772417

To Erika, Libby, and Amanda, the wonderful ladies at Edward Jones, and to my children with love.

To Die For

A MITCH COOPER Mystery

Chapter One

Mitch Cooper was on his second cup of coffee of the morning when the door to his office opened accompanied by the ringing of a small bell. He looked up to see a very exotic-looking woman stepping inside. She had very high cheekbones, almond-shaped eyes, a slightly up-turned nose and straight black hair. She wore a silver lame dress that hung on one shoulder and silver high-heeled sandals. She carried a small silver clutch purse as well.

"May I help you?" Cooper asked.

"I certainly hope so," the woman replied.

"I do too," Cooper grinned.

"My name is Paloma Verdes. My brother has disappeared and I want to hire you to find him," she said.

"How long has he been missing?" Cooper asked.

"Three days. The police have been no help at all," She told him.

"Three days is a long time. San Clemente is an hour away. Could your brother simply have parked his truck and walked away?"

"He could have, but I don't think that he did," Paloma said.

"Why is that?"

"I have a feeling."

"A feeling?" Cooper looked at her expectantly, waiting for more information. Most people are uncomfortable with long silences, and if you wait them out, most of the time they will start talking to fill the space.

"Enrico is a good boy, but far too trusting. He may be in real trouble. Please Mr. Cooper. I need your help!" she pleaded.

"Have you got a picture of him?" Cooper asked.

"Yes," Paloma replied, pulling it out of her purse and placing it on his desk. It was a picture that included her as well, and the family resemblance couldn't be argued. He had a feeling he was going to regret it, but he decided that he would take the case. He opened a drawer on his desk and pulled out a blank contract. He put it on the desk and looked at Paloma.

"I'm going to need you to sign a contract, which will make you my client and guarantees confidentiality. I charge $500.00 a day plus expenses and I need a three day retainer. If it takes longer than three days, I'll bill you for the additional time," Cooper explained.

"I'll write you a check," she replied. As Cooper began filling in the blanks on the standard contract form, Paloma pulled out a pink checkbook and opened it. She finished with the check and tore it out as he finished up the contract.

Cooper slid it across the desk for her to sign as he accepted the check, folding it and slipping it into his pocket. Once Miss Verdes had signed the contract, Cooper tore her copy off and handed it to her before putting his in a desk drawer. He then pulled out a legal pad and pen and put them on the desk.

"What is the name of the company your brother drives for?" Cooper asked, knowing he needed to gather some basic information so he could get started.

"Hi-Speed Delivery Service. He has worked for them for

the past two years, since he started going to San Diego State University," Paloma told him.

"Does he live on or off campus?"

"Off campus. Let me write down the address for you." Cooper pushed the pad across the desk to her. He could sense her quiet desperation for her missing brother. Paloma wrote the address down for him and gave him the pad back.

"You have good penmanship," he said, reading what she had written.

"Thanks," Paloma told him.

"I will find him, Miss Verdes. I just can't guarantee what shape he will be in when I do," Cooper said.

"I understand that, Mr. Cooper."

"Call me Mitch," he said.

"Okay, Mitch. Find my brother, please?"

"I'll do my best," he assured her. Cooper watched her get up and walk out the door. He appreciated the view as she was leaving. First, he was going to deposit the check in the bank. After that, he would run by the delivery service and see what Enrico's boss could tell him about the guy.

One lesson that Cooper had learned when he worked in Naval Intelligence is that information is the most valuable commodity in the world. He continued to apply that lesson as a private investigator. The more he could learn about Enrico Verdes, the more he could predict his movements and hopefully find out where he was. Cooper wasn't entirely sure that Paloma Verdes understood that. She was too embroiled in her emotional distress about her brother to listen to reason.

Paloma was concerned about her brother, and that was something Cooper could understand. However, it was also getting in the way of getting the necessary information to track her brother down. Cooper had a feeling that Enrico's boss, co-workers, or fellow tenants would know about Enrico's love life.

He had a feeling that Enrico wouldn't be the type to share details of his love life with an over-bearing sister like Paloma. No, Enrico would be more likely to keep any girlfriends a secret from her. He would be afraid that she would scare them off.

Cooper made a mental note to run checks on Paloma and Enrico both. He had both met and known women like Paloma Verdes before. They expected the world, no matter what the costs. Mitch Cooper knew one thing. Paloma Verdes was not a woman to die for, but one likely to get a man killed for her. He wondered if Enrico knew that about his sister.

~ ~ ~

Paloma Verdes frowned as she left Mitch Cooper's office. She felt that he had believed at least part of her story, but not all of it. That couldn't be avoided. But he had taken the job and he would start trying to find Enrico. That was what was important. It was what Julian had wanted.

Julian wanted to know what had happened to his cargo. The cargo that had been on the truck that Enrico was driving when he suddenly dropped off the grid. Why had Enrico done it? He should have known what Julian would do to him. It wouldn't matter to Julian that Enrico was her brother. Julian would kill him just the same. Unless Cooper found him first. If that happened, Paloma might have a chance to save her brother's life!

~ ~ ~

Enrico Verdes leaned back in his chair and took a long pull on his beer. The television was showing a baseball game featuring the Padres, but he really wasn't paying attention to it. He only had eyes for Giselle. She was a beauty. It had been her idea to ride along with him on this trip. Her idea to take the detour north of San Clemente to Dana Point and the vacation house that her parents owned.

Giselle was a beauty. She had long blonde hair and bright blue eyes. A sensuous mouth full of promise; and a body made for sin. Enrico was pretty sure that no ordinary man could resist her. On this day she was wearing a pair of high cut shorts and a pink halter top. She had three multi-colored jelly bracelets on each wrist. Her feet were bare, her toes painted the same coral shade as the nails on her hands. Her eyes were smoky with desire as she sat down on the couch beside him, her hands roving across his chest before encircling his neck and pulling his face down to hers for a long deep kiss.

Enrico kissed her back, feeling himself become aroused as he did so. Giselle was like no woman that he had ever met before. He didn't resist when he felt her hands on his belt, loosening it. Enrico didn't object as her fingers unfastened the button on his jeans and began working them and his underwear off his hips. He especially didn't fight when her hand encircled his member and her mouth lowered over it. At that point, Enrico quit thinking about anything...

~ ~ ~

Mitch Cooper walked through the front door of Hi-Speed Deliveries. A pretty brunette was at the front desk, her short hair pulled back into a small ponytail. She had on transparent blue-framed glasses. Pale pink lipstick coated

5

her lips. She wore a pale blue polo shirt with the company logo embroidered on the left front pocket. She looked up as he entered.

"Welcome to Hi-Speed Deliveries, how may I help you?" Her plastic name badge read Lara. Cooper offered her most winning smile.

"Well, Lara I was hoping to talk to your boss about one of your drivers," Cooper told her. Some of the warmth left her eyes.

"Do you have a complaint?" her voice had lost some of its welcome.

"Not at all. Do you get a lot of complaints?"

"No, but when we do, some of the people are really angry. One of them punched Leon in the mouth not two weeks ago because his delivery was broken inside the box. So I try to screen those people out," Lara explained.

"I promise I'm not here to hurt anyone, Lara. I just want to ask about one of the drivers that disappeared three days ago," Cooper explained.

"You mean Enrico," it was a statement more than a question.

"Yes. I'm a private investigator and his sister hired me to find him. Paloma's worried about him."

"His sister is a witch! She came in here one day and accused me of trying to seduce her brother away from her after Enrico took me out one night," Lara said.

"She struck me as being the over-protective sort," Cooper agreed.

"Over-protective my ass! She gets mad when she can't control Rico's every move and thought!"

"Sounds like you and Rico have talked about her?"

"We have, a lot. I like Rico, and if he took off to get away from her, more power to him. Give me a minute and I'll let Leon know you're here."

Cooper watched as Lara vanished through a doorway behind the counter. She had, he thought, a very nice walk. He could understand why Enrico had asked her out. What she had told him also matched his own impression of Paloma Verdes. He had already decided that if he found Enrico, he would give him a choice of whether or not he wanted Paloma to know about his whereabouts.

A few seconds later, Lara reappeared, followed by a tanned, white haired gentleman. Cooper assumed he was the Leon of who Lara had spoken earlier. "This is Mr. Cooper," she said. Cooper extended his hand across the counter and Leon shook it.

"You are?" Cooper asked.

"Leon DeGrassi. This is my company," the man replied.

"I'm looking for Enrico Verdes. His sister hired me to find him, and I understand that he works for you?" Cooper asked.

"He did. After him disappearing three days ago, and taking my truck full of deliveries with him, probably not," DeGrassi shrugged.

"Do you have a list of the deliveries that he was scheduled to make that day?"

"Probably back in my office. Lara, unlock the gate and let Mr. Cooper through."

"Sure thing, Leon," Lara replied as she threw the bolt and pulled part of the counter inward. Cooper stepped inside and Lara closed and locked the gate. Cooper followed DeGrassi back down the hall to his office.

"Did you know Enrico well?" Cooper asked as he took a seat in the chair across from DeGrassi.

"I thought I did," DeGrassi replied as he settled into his own chair.

"What about his sister, Paloma?"

"That is one nasty bitch kitty," DeGrassi sighed.

"Are you speaking from personal experience?" Cooper asked.

"I am," DeGrassi nodded.

"She came in here one time and verbally attacked Lara just because Rico took her out. After that, he made sure not to talk about anyone he was dating to his sister. Lara broke off her involvement with him after that," Leon shrugged.

"Do you know if Enrico was seeing anybody new?" Cooper asked.

Chapter Two

"Yeah, he had met some girl in a bar. Giselle something or other. I don't remember the last name but Rico was crazy over her. He said he couldn't let Paloma find out about her or she would ruin it, just like she had every other relationship he had been in," DeGrassi shrugged.

"You make it sound like Paloma and Enrico had a very unhealthy relationship," Cooper observed.

"Hell, they did have an unhealthy relationship. That woman is 100% batshit crazy where her little brother is concerned. I liked Rico, he was okay. Kind, fun-loving, a great guy. Until he stole my truck and disappeared," DeGrassi said.

"Yeah, that confirms my own impression of her," Cooper admitted.

"I'm not surprised. Listen, if you want to talk to the boys that's okay with me. If you find Rico, tell him I want my fucking truck back," DeGrassi said.

"Thanks. Are any of the other drivers in? Ones that were pals with Rico?"

"Yeah, Mateo and Stanley are in the garage loading up. I'll take you back." Cooper followed DeGrassi down the hall to the loading bay. There were two guys busy loading packages into two box trucks, One was a tall surfer type with tangled blonde hair and a wispy goatee, the other was a slender black kid with close cropped hair that looked like he worked out a lot. His arms were nearly as big around as his thighs. Cooper pegged the black kid as a power-lifter. He had the look.

"Ted, Beau, come on over here. This is Cooper. He's a P.I. looking for Rico," DeGrassi said by way of introduction.

"You a cop?" the black kid asked.

"Private. Paloma hired me to find her little brother," Cooper replied.

"That bitch be fucking crazy," Ted told him.

"I agree, but she is worried about her little brother."

"Dude, more than likely he's with Giselle. Rico was like totally hot for her. He said the sex was epic," Beau, the surfer added.

"Do either of you know anything about her?" Cooper asked.

"Not a lot, really," Ted shook his head.

"Do you know where he met her?"

"The Aero Club on India Street. Rico liked to hang out there," Ted said.

"Cool, maybe somebody at the club knows more about Giselle. Thank you," Cooper told them.

"Glad we could help," Beau shrugged as he gave Cooper a look.

"Anything helps," Cooper pulled out two of his cards and gave them each one. He gave DeGrassi one as well. "If you think of anything else, please call me."

Cooper headed back down the hallway towards the lobby. He was surprised when Lara grabbed his arm as he went past her.

"DeGrassi is connected, Cooper. He had a special shipment on that truck. He's being pressured to find Rico and turn him over to his boss."

"I thought DeGrassi owned the place."

"He's just the front man. This place is owned by the Mob. DeGrassi just fronts it to make it look legal," Lara whispered. Cooper slipped her one of his cards as well.

"Call me if you hear anything," he told her before exiting the office. Cooper walked to his GMC Sierra and climbed inside. Buckling his seatbelt, he fired the engine and pulled out of the parking lot.

This case was getting worse with every passing second. Cooper didn't like that the mob was involved. Things could get really hairy. He suspected that Paloma knew about the mob involvement. That was why she was so desperate that he found her brother first. Now it was starting to make sense.

Cooper headed for the address that Paloma had given him for her brother. The apartment was a small one bedroom unit on the second floor of the complex. A baseball cap and a clipboard made him look like any city utility worker around.

Using his picks, he was inside in less than a minute. It was a pretty Spartan bachelor's pad. Cooper closed the door behind him and headed for the bedroom. He figured that Enrico was the type that would make it the focus of the place when he was entertaining a lady. Entering the bedroom, he found that he was batting a thousand.

There was a wide screen television facing the bed and a DVR box next to it on the long and wide chest of drawers. Cooper made a note to check it out later. For the moment, he was more curious if Giselle had started keeping clothes at Rico's place. It turned out that she was. Cooper didn't learn a lot, just that Giselle favored thongs as her underwear of choice. He shook his head. Some women liked to dress with dental floss going up their ass.

~ ~ ~

Julian DiGeorgio stood looking out the window of his office, his hands clasped behind his back as he looked out over the city from the top floor of the high-rise building. DiGeorgio was tall and athletic, with wavy brown hair that he wore slicked back from a high forehead. He had a long aquiline nose, high cheek bones, and a strong, clean-shaved jaw. His eyes were brown and piercing. His suit was an Armani original. He looked every bit the picture of a successful business man.

He was concerned about the shipment that was supposed to have been delivered three days ago to Vinnie Calabresi. According to Vinnie, it had yet to arrive. Julian had assured Vinnie that he would make good on the shipment, no matter what. He didn't like being in that position. Paloma had assured him that using her brother and his job as a courier to move the drugs would be no problem. Julian was starting doubt Paloma and her assurances. If the drugs were not delivered in the next couple of hours, Julian would have no choice but to send men out to look for Paloma's brother.

They would not be kind or gentle once they found him, but they would find out where his shipment had gone astray. One way or another. His intercom buzzed. DiGeorgio turned and walked over to his desk and answered. "Yes?" he asked.

"Mister Falcone is here to see you," Greta, his secretary answered.

"Send him in," DiGeorgio said.

A moment later the door opened and 'Fast Eddie' Falcone walked into the office. Falcone was an enforcer for Vincent Calabresi, the head of the San Diego Mafia family. Falcone was always bad news. When Falcone appeared, the situation was usually about to go from bad to worse.

"Eddie, long time, no see," Julian said, putting on a welcoming smile. He extended his hand as Eddie shook it.

"Too long, Julian," Falcone smiled, acting all friendly.

"What can I do for you?" Julian asked.

"Vinnie is concerned, Julian. Vinnie is upset because he hasn't got his product. Vinnie says your delivery man flaked out and disappeared.

"Vinnie is exaggerating as usual. I've got boys out looking for Enrico Verdes as we speak."

"I hope so, Julian. Vinnie doesn't like losing money. He said to tell you that you'll need to make up for what he's already lost."

"Pleased let Vinnie know that I am handling it and that Vinnie will have his product within the next twenty-four hours. I'll also absorb the total cost so he isn't out any money for it," DiGeorgio said.

"I'll let him know," Falcone said as he turned and exited the office. Julian watched him leave. The door shut behind him. "Shit!" Julian snarled. He picked up the office phone and dialed the number for Mike Genovese from memory.

"Yeah?" Genovese answered.

"Find Enrico Verdes and find him right now! Do whatever it takes," Julian said.

"Sure thing, Boss," Genovese replied before hanging up. Julian dropped into his chair. It was bad enough losing the shipment, but now Vinnie was pissed and making waves. Rico was dead as soon as they found him and located the drugs. Paloma would just have to accept it, or she would die as well!

~ ~ ~

Cooper exited Rico's apartment and headed down the stairs to the parking lot. He wished he had more on Giselle than just her first name. It would make it easier to run a check on her and be helpful in locating her.

It was clear that Rico had met Giselle in a bar, but which one? The Aero Club? He would head there next. Maybe he would be able to find out more about Giselle. And her connection to Rico.

Cooper put the truck in drive and pulled away from the curb. The day was turning into a long one. Before long, Cooper knew he would have to go to San Clemente and start hunting for Rico up there. He hoped that he could find the kid before the mob headhunters did.

Cooper was not a fan of the mob. He never had been. He had dealt with them before, usually when they had targeted sailors to mule drugs for them when he was a part of Naval Intelligence. They were an unforgiving bunch. If Enrico Verdes was involved with them, he was in deep shit. And more than likely, his sister was the one that had gotten him involved with them.

Paloma Verdes entered the offices of Julian DiGeorgio. The receptionist gave her a cold look. Paloma entered DiGeorgio's office. Paloma's heart started beating faster. "Julian?" she asked, looking at him sitting at his desk.

"Paloma, we need to talk," Julian's gaze pinned her to the wall.

"About what?" she managed to force the words out.

"About your brother. He has disappeared. He has disappeared with the cargo that I trusted him with," DiGeorgio replied.

"What do you expect me to do about that?" Paloma asked.

"I expect you to find him for me," Julian told her.

"I am trying to do that," Paloma told him.

"Don't try, do it," Julian told her.

"I will do the best I can," Paloma said.

"Is that why you hired the private investigator to look for him?"

"It is."

"You worry me, Paloma," Julian said.

"I'm sorry for that," Paloma said.

"You understand my concerns?"

"I know that, Julian. I have done what I can to protect him, but I fear it is not enough," Paloma sighed.

"It never will be. Not everyone is good at being a spy."

"I thank you for that."

Chapter Three

Cooper arrived back at his office and parked the truck outside. He unlocked the door and headed to his desk. Cooper booted up his computer and typed the name Enrico Verdes into one of the special databases he had access to as an investigator. He opened another window and typed in Paloma Verdes, and typed Leon DeGrassi into another one, and then he sat back and waited. The searches would examine both police and public records for the names and would then provide all of the information available on the names.

Cooper got up and put on fresh coffee. It was more to kill time than anything else. Patience was one of the greatest skills that an investigator could possess. Cooper had it in abundance. He picked up the telephone and dialed a friend on the San Diego Police Department.

~ ~ ~

Renee Phillips answered the phone. "To what do I owe the pleasure, Cooper?"

"I'm working a missing person's case, and I was hoping you might be willing to help," Cooper told her.

"I'm special liaison to NCIS now, Mitch. You know that," Phillips replied.

"I do. I also know you still have connections in the department."

"I do. What exactly is it that you want?"

"I'm trying to find a guy named Enrico Verdes," Cooper

said.

"What has that got to do with me?" Phillips asked.

"His sister Paloma hired me. She said she filed a report. I want to find out if she really did."

"That sounds like a reasonable question. I'll find out and call you back."

"Thanks," Cooper told her and hung up.

~ ~ ~

Mike Genovese looked around at his crew. They had all worked for him for a long time. "We need to find Rico Verdes. He was the delivery driver that missed making the drop to Calabresi. He was last seen heading north towards San Clemente. He never dropped his package. The boss wants him dead or alive. It doesn't matter how as long as the package is recovered."

"Where should we start looking?" Vinnie Corolla asked.

"He was last seen heading for San Clemente, so I guess we should start looking going north. DeGrassi sent me over a print out of the kid's delivery schedule for that day. He said also that some private dick has been around asking about Rico, so we need to find the kid first," Genovese said.

"So what's the plan?" Corolla asked.

"I've made a list of stops for each team to check out. Vito has them," Genovese replied.

~ ~ ~

Cooper looked up as the first search engine beeped, letting it know that it had something. Not surprisingly, it was the search he had entered for DeGrassi. DeGrassi was in the Mafia, a full blown made man. He had numerous arrests for assault and battery, a few for shylocking, one or two for running numbers, and was suspected in half a dozen murders, but never convicted. His arrests stopped after he opened the delivery service.

Cooper could guess why. DeGrassi had to keep his nose clean because drugs and weapons were likely moving through his business as well as a front for money laundering. Poor Enrico was in more danger than his sister had let on. Cooper pulled out a legal pad and made notes.

DeGrassi was bad news. And if Rico had screwed him over, then more than likely, Rico Verdes was going to die. That meant that Cooper had to find him fast!

He wished that he had a better idea of where the kid was hiding. He wondered if Paloma knew how much trouble that her little brother was in. He thought that she might, but he also knew that she was hiding things from him. Cooper wanted to know what those things might be.

The computer beeped again and Cooper got a good look at Paloma Verdes. Paloma had immigrated to America from Mexico and she had done it the right way. She had come on a visa and had applied for citizenship, taking the classes and passing the tests. She had been given citizen ship less than a decade ago. She had built a reputation as a model, and worked hard at it. She had made the covers of several local magazines for her exotic beauty.

She also had a few arrests for prostitution. At some point, she had come to the attention of one Julian DiGeorgio. DiGeorgio was a well-known Mobster and the head of the San Diego Mafia Family. Cooper leaned back in his chair as he digested this information.

One thing he was sure of, poor old Rico was royally and truly fucked! If his sister was tight with DiGeorgio, it was likely that DiGeorgio had picked him to make a special delivery. Since that delivery had not been made, DiGeorgio would be sending people after him. Shit!

Cooper was beginning to wish he had not agreed to take the case. However, the check had cleared and he had already started. So he had to see it through to the very end.

It was not a good thing. It could get him killed, but that was just part of the job. Cooper would do what he could, but he hadn't made any promises.

Sighing, Cooper opened his desk drawer and pulled out his Beretta Px4 Storm 9mm. He was sure he was going to need it on this case. First, he needed to find out more about the mysterious girlfriend, Giselle. It was time, he decided, to check out the Aero Club. But he needed to stop by his house first. The club would require that he take on another persona, a cover legend.

~ ~ ~

Cooper was driving his red Mitsubishi Eclipse Sport as he approached the Aero Club. While it was well known as a dive bar since 1947, and for having 800 different brands of whiskey available, it had become something of a place where the local upscale hipsters liked to hang out.

Cooper had a sports coat on over his polo shirt and Khakis, to cover the gun holstered on his hip. He had spare magazines in both pockets, just in case he needed them. If Rico had met Giselle here, Cooper could hopefully find somebody that knew her.

Finding out about Giselle was important. It was obvious that Rico was head and heels over her. The question was had he been targeted by her? Or was it an honest relationship? Given the fact that Paloma was tied to Julian DiGeorgio; the targeting felt like it was the better choice of the two. There was also the fact that Rico had fallen for her so quickly. That seemed to indicate that he had been targeted specifically.

Cooper pulled into the parking lot and shut off the Eclipse's engine. He opened the door and stepped out into the late afternoon heat. It was after five, so he figured this would be about the time that Rico would have stopped in to get a drink on the way home from his delivery job. Cooper had a picture of Enrico that he could show around. Somebody might remember him, especially if Giselle had fixated on him. Any man a beautiful woman fixated on would be a topic of discussion. It was human nature.

Guys would wonder what he had that they didn't, and the women would wonder what it was that he had that made him so special to her. It would be a topic of conversation. From what Cooper knew of Rico, he had average good looks, but Giselle was far above his league.

Cooper pushed open the glass door and stepped into the coolness of the club. The place was already packed and Cooper fought his way to the bar. He ordered Jim Beam and smiled at the girl behind the bar.

"Here you go," she said, putting the glass on the bar in front of him. "Your first time here?" she asked.

"It is. A friend told me about this place. You might know him, Enrico Verdes?" Cooper looked into her eyes. She blinked twice.

"We all know Rico. He's a fun guy," she shrugged. Her name tag read Rhonda.

"Popular with the ladies?" Cooper asked her.

"He used to be. Until he met Giselle," Rhonda replied.

"Tell me about Giselle," Cooper prompted.

21

"Giselle made all the girls jealous, especially when she set her sights on Rico."

"Why was that?"

"Like you said, he was a popular guy with the ladies."

"Can you describe Giselle?"

"Tall, blonde, blue eyes, kind of like Farrah Fawcett back in the day. She was a looker. She hadn't been around here until about a month ago. Then one night after Rico came in, she showed up and she set her sights on him from the minute she walked through the door." Rhonda said as she wiped down the bar with a wet rag.

"Would you say that she was targeting Rico?" Cooper asked.

"That's a good way of putting it. It was like she came in looking for him."

"Why do you think she would do that?"

"It was like she knew he would be here that night, and she was going to make sure that he left with her," Rhonda said, a troubled look on her face.

"Any idea why she might do that?" Cooper asked.

"None. Rico worked for a delivery service, basically he drove a truck and dropped off packages."

"So what interest could Giselle possibly have in a glorified mail man?" Cooper asked.

"We all wondered about that," Rhonda nodded.

"So what did you decide?"

"We never could agree. Nobody could figure it out."

"Do you know what Giselle's last name might be?" Cooper asked.

"Yes, because I checked her ID the first time she came in here. Giselle Haskell."

"Do you happen to remember the address on the ID?"

"Not the street, but it was from San Clemente," Rhonda said.

"Thank you, Rhonda. Rico has disappeared and he has some bad people looking for him. I want to get to him first, and get him out from under those bad people," Cooper explained.

"Is Giselle part of those bad people?" Rhonda looked into his eyes.

"I think so," Cooper replied honestly.

"Then you find Rico and help him. He doesn't deserve for anything bad to happen to him."

"I agree with you, Rhonda. And I'll do my best to help him."

"I believe you. If you can help him, I hope you'll come back again. I like you."

"I like you too," Cooper told her, tossing a $10.00 on the bar as he drained his drink and left.

Sweat was beading on his brow as he stepped outside. The quiet was a welcome change from the noise levels inside. The two fingers of Jim Beam was spreading through his body. The cool night air was drying the sweat as it came out.

He had a full name on Giselle Haskell, something that he didn't have before. Now he needed to find out who she really was, and who she might be working for.

Cooper was almost back to his car when the big guy came out of the shadows and gave him a bum's rush. Cooper had caught the movement out of the corner of his eye, but it was enough to allow him to spin and drive a foot into the attacker's gut. The guy folded like a cheap suit before hitting the ground.

Cooper stepped in and caught the guy by the back of his shirt and jerked him up-right, the collar of his shirt choking him slightly. Cooper pulled his gun and drove it into the man's gut, angling the muzzle upwards towards his heart.

"Who the fuck are you?" Cooper demanded. The guy was still gasping for air. He extended his hands far out to the sides. Cooper thumbed back the hammer, letting the guy hear the click as the pistol cocked.

"You need to back off, Cooper," the man gasped.

"And why is that?" Cooper asked, taking up the slack on the trigger.

"Because you don't know what the hell you are getting involved in," the guy said.

"And you do?" Cooper asked.

"You start fucking around in this, you will get yourself killed," the man said.

"Really? And you know this how?" Cooper asked him.

Chapter Four

Enrico Verdes opened his eyes. He wasn't sure if it was day or night. Giselle had that effect on him. When he was with her, it was like he had stepped out of time. Such a woman! He had never known anyone like her in his life. He lifted his left wrist and looked at his watch. 10:00 p.m. Wow, he had really been out of it. Giselle was no longer in bed with him, so she must have awakened earlier. Rico rolled to a sitting position on the edge of the bed. He rubbed the sleep out of his eyes and reached for a plastic bottle of water, unscrewing the cap and taking a long pull that drained nearly half of it. He put the cap back on and got up and made his way to the bathroom.

Five minutes later, business taken care of, he found his underwear and pulled them on, then his pants, and then he walked out into the living room. Still no sign of Giselle? Where the hell was she? He shook his head as he drained the rest of the bottle of water. She probably left to go get them some food. Rico dropped into a chair and scooped the television remote from the coffee table and clicked on the TV.

There was little of interest on so he turned it to the local news. He was surprised to see the date was three days later! Where had the time gone? Shit, he was in big fucking trouble. DeGrassi had told him to make that special delivery the day he had left San Diego, had said it was time sensitive! Enrico stood and walked back to the bedroom and finished getting dressed. He had to get his truck and make that delivery if he did nothing else!

Where the fuck was Giselle? He didn't know but he couldn't afford to wait on her either. He had to get to his truck. He walked out of the house. His truck was missing! Rico began to panic. What the hell had happened? The warehouse. He had forgotten that they had parked the truck there so that nobody would find it. Paloma would hate him; and DeGrassi would fucking kill him for losing the truck! He was in deep shit!

~ ~ ~

Mitch Cooper ran Giselle Haskell through his search engines on his home computer. It had the same software as the one at the office. He had a bad feeling about this girl, and an even worse one about Rico. The kid was neck deep in a shithole and it wasn't his fault. He had no clue that his sister had set him up.

It was times like this that Cooper wished he smoked, because it would at least give him something to do. He didn't, so he would have to calm himself by other means. He dropped a CD into the drive on his computer and it began playing something by Lex Baker. Baker was an old timer who wrote jazz soundtracks for old movie scores. It helped Cooper relax.

~ ~ ~

Renee Phillips frowned as she read the report on Enrico Verdes. For the most part, the guy was clean, though his sister had some pretty questionable relationships. His sister was a different story all together. She had multiple arrests on her record. She was also tied to the San Diego Mafia family. Phillips sighed, knowing that there was a good chance that she would need to let her current boss, Gabriel King, know about what was going on.

King was the lead NCIS officer out of the San Diego offices.

He was not a fan of Mitch Cooper. The two of them had a bad history, one that colored Kings view of any case that Cooper was involved in. Narcotics smuggling was a big problem in San Diego, especially given the fact that it sat right on the border with Mexico. The drug cartels and the Mafia worked together to bring poison across the border and spread it out across the country.

Renee Phillips dialed Cooper's cell number. "Cooper," he answered on the first ring.

"That guy you asked me to check out? Verdes? He's got mob ties through his sister. They are connected to Julian DiGeorgio's outfit," Phillips said.

"Swell," Cooper replied. Phillips could almost hear his eyes rolling.

"You were the one that came to me, friend. Not the other way around," Phillips reminded him.

"I know that, Renee. Okay, thank you," Cooper told her.

"Hey, be careful Cooper. If this involves drugs, King is going to get involved if you like it or not."

"Gabriel King has always been a pushy bastard. I'll deal with him when the time comes. I gotta go," Cooper told her before ending the call. Phillips looked at the telephone in her hand for a long moment before hanging it up as well. She hoped that Cooper knew what he was doing.

~ ~ ~

Giselle Haskell sat across from the guy she knew as Mike. Mike was tall and dark, deeply tanned skin, brown hair and cold blue eyes. Mike was wearing a pale blue polo shirt and tan khakis and brown loafers. His was obviously strong, with wide shoulders and narrow hips. Handsome too.

"So how is our boy doing?" Mike asked.

"He was sleeping when I left. I need to get back before he wakes up," Giselle shrugged.

"Does he know you brought me that 'special' delivery he was carrying for DiGeorgio?" Mike asked.

"Once I get him started, he forgets about everything," Giselle said, sticking her tongue out and running it across her lips. Mike barked out a harsh-sounding laugh.

"I bet he does, Sweetheart. Okay, get back to the kid and keep him occupied until morning. By then, this whole deal will be over and there might even be a bonus in it for you," Mike told her. He tossed a twenty onto the table and walked out of the small dinner. Giselle watched him go, wondering if she had done the right thing by substituting the package he had thought she was giving him for another one. Well, too late for second thoughts now. She headed for her own car and drove back to the house where she and Rico were staying.

Something was different when she pulled up to the house. It took her a moment to realize what it was. The rental car that they had driven from the place where they had stashed the truck was gone! Giselle jumped out of the car and ran inside. Where the hell was Rico?

~ ~ ~

The sun was going down as Cooper made himself a cold turkey sandwich on whole wheat bread with mayo and lettuce. A glass of cold milk topped off his dinner. He needed to head for San Clemente very soon and see if he could pick up Enrico Verdes' trail. Julian DiGeorgio would have people out looking for the poor dumb kid, and the kid had no idea how big a shithole that he had stepped in.

Normally, he preferred to us the GMC pickup when he was working, but he had a feeling that he might need the maneuverability and all out speed that the Eclipse would give him, not to mention the spare pistol and magazines under the driver's seat in the safe.

Cooper finished off the last bite of his sandwich and drained the rest of his milk to wash it down. He rinsed off the dishes and put them in the dishwasher before heading to his room to pack the things that he thought he might need.

~ ~ ~

Rico parked the rental car outside the old warehouse where they had hidden the delivery truck. The longer he was away from Giselle, the more he regretted being so impulsive and running off with her. He would be lucky if he still had a job when he got back down to San Diego. He shook his head, knowing that Mr. DeGrassi was going to be pissed!

And that wasn't even the worst of it! Paloma would never let him out of her sight again! He loved his older sister, but she was so suffocating when it came to him. He wished that she would just let him live his life and not always be trying to protect him. He realized that it was because she loved him and wanted the best for him, but at twenty-three years old, he needed his freedom to meet life on his terms, something that Paloma refused to understand.

Rico shook his head as he pushed open the door to the

abandoned warehouse. Thank God, the truck was right where he had left it. It was getting late, but he would come up with some kind of story to explain his tardiness. He walked around the truck, inspecting it. It looked good, and he breathed a sigh of relief. Giselle was probably going to be pissed that he had left, but he would deal with that after he made the rest of his deliveries.

~ ~ ~

Mike reached his motel room and tossed the package onto the bed. Giselle was some piece of work. He shook his head, wondering just where the hell the boss had found her. The important thing was that he had recovered the package.

Mike opened the small fridge in the room and pulled out a tray of ice cubes and a bottle of Jim Beam. He sat them on the desk and tore the plastic wrap off of the plastic cup. He added a couple of cubes of ice and then poured two fingers of whiskey over it. He took a sip, enjoying the burn as it slid down his throat into his belly. He could have been at home, but didn't want to take a chance on that crazy broad finding out where he lived.

Mike pulled his pocket knife out and flicked the blade open and walked to the package and cut it open. He folded the blade in and dropped it back in his pocket before opening the box. His face flushed red as he saw what was in it and he hurled the box against the wall. A stuffed animal tumbled out onto the floor.

Mike snatched up his cell phone and dialed the boss. The fucking girl had betrayed them!

~ ~ ~

Eddie Falcone frowned as he watched the news. It was bad. But then the news usually was. Two young girls had been murdered in Indiana of all places. He had been there once. Indiana was a quiet place. Shit like that normally didn't happen there. He shut off the television, cutting Inside Edition short.

He needed to concentrate on this fuck up of DiGeorgio's. Calabresi was pissed that he still didn't have his drugs, and that was all on Deej. He never should have trusted the girl's brother, even if he did work for Leon. Now, Eddie was going to have to clean the whole thing up. That was what Calabresi paid him for.

Eddie picked up the room phone and dialed a number. "Hello?" asked a voice at the other end.

"Find and scrub Enrico Verdes. Vinnie wants it done yesterday."

"Sure thing Eddie," the voice replied, and then the connection was ended. Eddie took a drink of Scotch as he put the telephone down. Tomorrow would be another fucking day.

~ ~ ~

Cooper was on the move. San Clemente was only an hour away and the Eclipse would cut down on the time. The sleek red car was fast and handled good. Cooper was worried about Enrico Verdes. The kid had no idea what he had stepped in.

Cooper felt sorry for Rico. He hoped that he would find the kid in time to pull him out of the mess that his sister had gotten him into. He had his laptop in a carrying case fastened into the seat belt on the passenger seat. He also had a 12-guage Mossberg pump shotgun with a pistol grip and extra rounds in the trunk of the speedy sports car as well. The radar detector on the dash allowed him to run about ten miles over the speed limit on his way north. He figured that might help any run-ins with the police.

~ ~ ~

Mike was on the move as well, and he was hunting Giselle. The girl had fucked him and his people over. She was now a liability. He figured if he found her, he would find Rico Verdes, and if he found Rico, he would find the actual package.

He had called the boss and let him know as well. He hadn't been happy. It had fucked up his plans, but he left it to Mike to fix it.

~ ~ ~

Rico drove to the places that were open and made the deliveries, apologizing for the delay and putting it down to engine trouble. Most of the places accepted what he told them at face value. A few of them grumbled and said they weren't happy and that his boss had better make it up to them the next time around. Rico had promised that they would. It was an empty promise, but the shop owners didn't know that. It was only once he had dropped off the last package on the truck that he realized that there were two packages missing. One was to a private residence. The other was the special package that was addressed to a Mr. Calabresi. The special package that DeGrassi had entrusted him with. Shit! He wondered if Giselle had swiped it. If she had, he was as good as dead!

Chapter Five

Giselle was frantic as she searched the house. Rico wasn't there! Where had he gone? The warehouse where they had parked the delivery truck. That had to be where he had gone. He didn't know that she had removed and swapped the two packages from the truck. He had no idea of the danger he was in! Giselle pulled out her cell phone and dialed Rico's number, praying that he would answer.

The sun was sinking over the Pacific as she raced out of the house to her car. She jumped inside and fired the engine, fastened her seatbelt, and then peeled out of the driveway.

~ ~ ~

"Rico," he said as he answered his cell phone. He recognized the number as Giselle. There had been a ton of missed calls from his sister. He had ignored those. He couldn't ignore Giselle. She was like a highly addictive drug to him.

"Where the hell are you, Rico?" she asked, her tone angry.

"Finishing up my delivery schedule. I'm short two packages. Do you know anything about that?" he asked, his voice sounding upset.

"Yes," Giselle replied contritely.

"You know that I am probably going to lose my job over this?" Rico asked her, letting his own anger color the question.

"I know, Rico and I am sorry," Giselle told him.

"I actually believe you. Do you know how much trouble I am in?" Rico asked.

"More than you know," Giselle replied.

"You think? Giselle, I am going to lose my job, and then I'll have to move back in with my sister. I can't do that again," Rico said petulantly.

"Believe me, Rico, Paloma is going to be the least of your troubles if we can't get away from here!"

"What are you talking about?" Rico asked, catching the sound of fear in her voice.

"There is this guy named Mike, and he asked me to steal one of your packages. That special delivery you were making for Mr. DiGeorgio. I made him think I did it, but by now he knows I double-crossed him. He's going to come after us and kill us both," Giselle explained.

"Aw fuck, Giselle! Why did you do that? Do you have any idea who Mr. DiGeorgio is?" Rico asked her.

"No," she replied.

"He's part of the goddam Mafia! You are right, we need to get the hell gone or we are both dead!"

"I'm so sorry, Rico. I was just trying to get us enough money to go away."

"I'll meet you at the warehouse. I gotta dump this truck as quick as I can. Go to the warehouse and wait!" Rico said before hanging up. Giselle put her face in her hands and wept.

It was getting dark as Cooper reached San Clemente. Some of the businesses that Rico was supposed to deliver to

were open. He figured it would be worth checking to see if
Rico had made his deliveries, even if he was late.

The problem with trying to find somebody when they
were on the run was that usually they would go off the grid,
use burner phones, and cash, knowing that their credit or
debit cards could be traced along with their regular cell
phones. Cooper had to hope that Rico and his girlfriend
weren't that smart. But the bad part, the bad guys could
track them the same way!

Cooper had plugged the first stop into his GPS and
swung to the curb. He was in luck, the store was still open.
Cooper locked his car before heading into the store. The
Eclipse was one of the cars that car thieves looked for. They
were sleek and sporty and would bring good money south
of the border or overseas. He also activated the anti-theft
system.

Grangers Automotive was a parts place. Cooper shoved
open the door and walked inside. There were two or three
customers in the store and four or five employees. Cooper
made his way to the counter and asked for the manager.

He was surprised when a young redhead girl came out
from the back. She had a nice build, enough so that he was
interested. The name on her name tag read Charlotte.
"What can I do for you, Sir?" she asked. She had a slight
southern accent, more Texas than California.

"My name is Mitch Cooper and I'm a private
investigator. I'm looking for the deliveryman from Hi Speed
Deliveries. Has he been in over the past couple of days?"
Cooper asked her.

"Call me Charlie. Charlotte is way too formal. Yeah,
Rico was a couple of days late, but he dropped off our parts

today," she told him.

"How long ago?" Cooper asked.

"A couple of hours ago."

"That helps."

"I hope so," she smiled at him. She had a pretty smile.

"Believe me it does," Cooper smiled back, and then he turned and headed back out the door. Two minutes later he was back in his car and heading north.

The next place that was open was on the north end of town, out towards Dana Point. Cooper headed that way.

~ ~ ~

Arty Grimaldi and Benny Giacomo spotted the truck heading north. Benny was driving so Arty called Genovese. "We got him," Arty said.

"Grab him and bring his ass back to San Diego. Mr. DiGeorgio wants to talk to him. His life depends on it," Genovese replied.

"Sure thing, Mr. Genovese. We'll be on his ass until he stops and then we'll put the grab on him and bring him back," Arty said.

~ ~ ~

Rico was getting close to the warehouse. He hoped that Giselle was there waiting because they were going to have words about the shitstorm she had managed to call down on them. It was about that time that he noticed the black Lincoln Continental that was coming up fast behind him.

The black car was running right up on his tail. Too goddam close. He saw a face that he recognized as one of Julian DiGeorgio's boys behind the wheel. Oh Fuck me running. He stomped on the gas and pushed the pedal to the floor. The delivery van leapt forward. Rico glanced at the speedometer. It was climbing. Sixty-five, seventy miles per hour. Seventy-five, eighty. Eighty-five, ninety miles per hour. The whole damn van was shaking like it was about to fly apart.

The black Lincoln was staying right with him, trying to get around him. Enrico swung the van out, blocking them, keeping them from being able to get alongside him. It was then he heard a rattling sound, like hail hitting the vehicle. The bastards were shooting at him! Rico maneuvered until they were directly behind him and then he slammed on the brakes, bracing for the nearly instant impact as the Lincoln hit the heavy steel rear bumper of the truck. The Lincoln folded like an accordion, shoving g the engine back into the front seat and catching fire. Rico put the van in low gear and pulled away from the shattered and burning Lincoln. The front bumper of the car pulled off and dragged for a few feet behind him before falling off.

Rico headed for the warehouse. He had to get there quick and then get the hell gone from the area. If DiGeorgio was hunting him, he was as good as dead if he was caught!

~ ~ ~

Mitch Cooper spotted the van and the chase car instants before the van braked and the Lincoln hit it. He hit his own brakes and skidded to a halt in time to see the van pull free and the Lincoln blow up as the flames hit the fumes from a broken gas line. The van took off again, not bothering to check on the shattered Lincoln. Cooper could pretty well guess what that meant. He hit the gas and headed after the van, but staying far enough back that the same thing couldn't happen to him. He could guess that the guys in the Lincoln belonged to Julian DiGeorgio. Which meant the

Enrico Verdes now had an idea of the trouble that he was in.

Cooper didn't know if that made his job easier or harder. He hoped it would make it easier. He had to convince the kid that he wasn't working for DiGeorgio or whoever was trying to take DiGeorgio on.

He felt sorry for the kid. He didn't want to turn him over to his sister, which meant turning him over to DiGeorgio. He had to convince the kid and figure out a way to keep him safe.

Cooper stayed back, following the van from a distance. He would see where it went and go from there. He had not planned on getting involved in a mob war, but it appeared that might be exactly what was happening!

~ ~ ~

Giselle looked up as the door to the warehouse started to lift. She wiped the tears from her eyes as Rico drove the van inside and the door started to close. "Thank God," she whispered. Rico pulled the van to a stop and shut off the engine. A moment later, he opened the door and stepped outside. Giselle ran to him and threw her arms around him.

"Oh Rico, I am so glad to see you!" Giselle cried.

"How long, Giselle?" Rico asked.

"What do you mean?" Giselle asked.

"How long have you been playing me?" Rico grabbed her upper arms and looked into her eyes.

"I haven't been," Giselle replied, meeting his gaze.

"Then why did you take the special package?"

"Because Mike said he would kill me if I didn't."

"You said that you didn't give it to him on the phone."

"That's right, I didn't. And by now he knows that."

"So Mike is after us too?" Rico asked.

"Yeah," Giselle hung her head and sobbed.

"You are going to get us fucking killed, Giselle! Did you realize that?" Rico yelled.

"She had no idea," said a tall, good looking blond guy as he stepped out from behind the van.

"Just who the hell are you?" Rico demanded.

"My name is Mitch Cooper. I'm a private investigator and I am here to help you," the man said.

"Prove it," Rico snarled.

"For one thing, you are still alive. If I was working for DiGeorgio, you wouldn't be."

"That sounds reasonable."

"It should, because it is the truth. Your sister hired me to find you," Cooper explained.

"Why? So she could turn me over to her boss?" Rico asked.

"No. I think because she truly is worried about you. The thing with DiGeorgio is secondary," Cooper explained.

"Then what the fucking hell am I supposed to do?" Rico asked.

"Do you have the package for Calabresi?" Cooper asked.

"How the fuck do you know about that?"

"Your sister told me."

"You will have to ask Giselle. She was the one that stole it," Rico said bitterly. Cooper looked at the young woman.

"Do you have it?" Cooper asked her.

"I know where it is," Giselle admitted.

"Then you need to tell me so I can make sure that it reaches Calabresi," Cooper told her.

"Why should I believe you?" Giselle demanded.

"I can drive back down to San Diego and let DiGeorgio or that guy Mike kill you both. I collect my money either way. I am trying to help you both," Cooper explained.

"Can you really keep us alive?" Rico asked.

"I can try," Cooper told him. Rico looked at Giselle. "What will Mike do?" he asked.

"He will kill us both since I gave him the wrong package," Giselle admitted.

"I am the best chance you both have," Cooper told them.

"As much as I hate it, I have to agree," Rico sighed.

"So what do we do?" Rico asked.

"Both of you come with me and I will see what the hell I can do to keep you from getting killed," Cooper told them.

Chapter Six

San Diego, California.

Julian DiGeorgio frowned as he looked into his drink, as if he could see bad news lurking beneath the dark red surface of the wine. There had been no word from the people that Genovese had sent to look for Enrico Verdes. Paloma was quiet as she sat curled up on the love seat across the room from him, watching some silly comedy called of all things, Jane the Virgin. Women! Who knew what they would find interesting or amusing.

With men, DiGeorgio knew where he stood. They feared and respected him. But a woman? No man could read tracks on the barren soil of a woman's heart!

"You look troubled, my love," Paloma said softly from where she sat. She also had a half empty glass of wine in her hand.

"I am, Paloma. You know why," he replied, and then took a sip of his wine.

"I haven't heard from Rico either. I am worried Julian. He is my baby brother and very naïve in the ways of the world," Paloma confessed.

"Perhaps he is not as naïve as you might think, Paloma. My friend Leon gave him a job and looked out for him. Gave him honest work so he could earn a living. How did Enrico repay him? He stole an entire truckload of packages and disappeared. Enrico is nothing more than a dirty thief!" DiGeorgio roared in anger.

"He is not a thief!" Paloma screamed back at him. "It was that tramp of a girl that he started seeing. I am sure that she is behind this!"

"Paloma, you are jealous of any woman that Enrico shows interest in. Are you sure that you don't want him for yourself? Is that it? You want to fuck your brother like the gutter whore you were before I found you?" DiGeorgio asked softly, yet his tone was even more menacing. All of the blood left Paloma's face. She did not like being reminded of her past.

"No, Julian. I had promised my mother that I would watch over him. However when a young boy starts thinking with his penis, his brain is no longer in control," Paloma replied contritely.

"On that, we agree. Your brother has cost me a great deal, not only money, but prestige within the Family. Calabresi is not the forgiving sort, and he cares little for affairs of the people under him. He only looks at the bottom line and the flow of dollars into his coffers. Money is his God." DiGeorgio explained.

"Is money the only God that you worship, Julian?" Paloma asked. She took a sip of her wine as well.

"You know it is not, Paloma. Money is what gives me this house and puts the clothing on your back. Money from the Family business. Have you heard from the private investigator that you hired to find Enrico?"

"How did you know about that?"

"I know every move that you make Paloma. I am not so infatuated with you that I am not careful. You can be replaced at any time, Paloma. There are many women who would gladly take your place."

"That is so, Julian. I know this. No, I have not heard anything back from Mitch Cooper."

"You will tell me when you do?"

"I will," Paloma promised.

~ ~ ~

Gabriel King was looking through the files on his desk. He was alone in the NCIS squad room, everyone else having gone home for the night. He leaned back in his chair and pulled up a file on his computer. The file was on a San Diego Mafia boss named Julian DiGeorgio. DiGeorgio was the man when it came to smuggling drugs into San Diego. A lot of times, he liked to use sailors to do his dirty work. Or Marines.

That was something that King hated. King had been a Marine before joining NCIS. Marines were dying from smuggling dope from Mexico into the United States, not just from the Cartels, but from the Mafia as well. Some of them were trying to pay off loan sharks that they had gotten south of through gambling or other vices. Julian DiGeorgio was the man in control.

He was also number one on Gabriel King's personal list of the ten most wanted criminals in San Diego. King started reading the latest intel reports on DiGeorgio.

~ ~ ~

Mitch Cooper took the pair back to Giselle's place on Dana Point. He looked at the girl. He could see why Rico was so smitten with her. He could also see the predatory look hiding in her eyes. Giselle had her own agenda. Cooper could see it even if Rico couldn't. He got out of the car and followed the young couple inside.

"Where is it?" Rico glared at Giselle.

"The bedroom," Giselle replied, trying to sound contrite. Cooper didn't buy it for a moment. Giselle was out for herself and nobody else. He stayed with her as Rico headed for the bedroom.

"I hope you are telling him the truth."

"I am," Giselle said.

"You better be," Cooper told her.

Rico reappeared from the bedroom holding a box in both of his hands.

"Is that it?" Cooper asked.

"It had better be," Rico said as he glared at Giselle.

"Any idea what it contains?" Cooper asked.

"No," Rico replied. Cooper looked at Giselle.

"Well?" he asked. Giselle looked away.

"Giselle, if you know, you had better tell him," Rico said.

"I—," she started and then fell silent.

"Giselle, I love you, but I am not going to die for you or because of you. If you know what is in this fucking box you had damn well better spill it!" Rico snarled angrily.

"Okay, okay!" Giselle said, showing her own anger at being ganged up on by the two men.

"We're waiting," Cooper told her.

"Its drugs, at least that is what Mike told me. Some guy named Eddie wanted to stir up trouble between DiGeorgio and Calabresi," Giselle sighed.

"How did you meet this Mike?" Cooper asked.

"Why do you want to know?" she glared at him.

"Because at the moment I don't know. The more I know, the easier it will be to figure out a way to keep the both of you alive," Cooper replied.

"You do want to live, don't you?" Rico asked her.

"Yes, I do," Giselle sighed, looking defeated.

~ ~ ~

Renee Phillips was asleep when her telephone rang. It dragged her out of a good dream and she didn't appreciate it one bit. "Yes?" she asked.

"Get your ass to the office," Gabriel King told her.

"What's up?" Renee asked.

"I think we may have a fucking mob war brewing," King told her.

"Shit!"

"Pretty much."

Phillips rolled out of bed, pulling her nightgown off over her head and throwing it at the laundry hamper. Naked, she headed for the bathroom to take care of business and grab a shower. Renee Phillips was an attractive woman and she knew it. Sometimes she played to that during interrogations. It was one of her weapons and she wasn't above using it. Not if it brought the case to a conclusion.

Part of her wondered if it had anything to do with the call she had received from Cooper earlier in the day. If it did, she would have to tell King about it, and King would not be happy. The whole adversarial relationship between the two men bothered her. She liked and respected both of them, and she knew that they respected each other. The level of dislike was like nothing she had ever encountered before.

Renee knew that it involved a young female Marine that Cooper was training in Navy Intelligence, and she knew that the young woman had died. She also knew that Cooper blamed King for getting her killed. But she had a feeling that there was more to it on a personal level that neither man would talk about.

She turned on the hot water in the shower as she sat on the toilet and did her thing. Once she was done, she flushed and climbed into the shower and washed her hair and conditioned it before washing her body. She stepped out, wrapped her hair in a towel, and then dried off her body. She walked out to get dressed, the towel still on her head.

~ ~ ~

Mike Genovese frowned. He hadn't heard from Arty or Benny since they had called in to say they had spotted the kid. That didn't bode well. Julian wasn't happy, and correspondingly, that meant that Genovese wasn't happy. His crew knew that. That was why the few that weren't on the hunt were walking on egg shells around him.

He knew that Julian was under a lot of fucking pressure from Eddie Falcone. Calabresi was a fucking asshole, but he ranked higher than DiGeorgio in the family hierarchy at the moment. He wondered if finding the kid would really help. Falcone gave him a bad feeling.

Genovese picked up the phone and dialed Vencenzio. Vencenzio was a free-lancer. Murder for hire. Fast Eddie Falcone was becoming a real problem for Mister DiGeorgio. Genovese felt like it was time to start removing some of his boss's problems. "Vito, come over. I have a job for you," he said when Vencenzio answered. "Thanks, Vito. I'll see you soon."

~ ~ ~

Gabriel King looked impatient when Renee Phillips walked into the bullpen. "Took you long enough," he said grumpily.

"Well, I was asleep when you called, and since it is after midnight, I needed to stop for coffee on the way over here," Phillips told him as she entered her cubicle and dropped her purse to the floor. She had put on a pale blue cotton blouse and was wearing a charcoal gray pants suit with black heels.

"I keep forgetting you were a civilian cop and never in the service," King sighed.

"Might be a good time to start remembering," she told him dropping into her chair. "So what is this about a mob war?" she asked.

"Somebody ripped off Julian DiGeorgio. Took a package full of dope, and the entire truck complete with driver," King said.

"Any idea who?" Phillips asked.

"According to the Organized Crime Unit, it was intended for Vinnie Calabresi. Fast Eddie Falcone is his top enforcer and he met with DiGeorgio earlier today," King replied.

"So where do we come in?" Phillips asked.

"We have an undercover officer in DiGeorgio's camp. He got in because DiGeorgio was selling to sailors and Marines," King replied.

"Do we have anything on the delivery driver?" Phillips asked.

"Enrico Verdes, brother to Julian DiGeorgio's main squeeze, Paloma Verdes. You're going to like this part. She hired your buddy Mitch Cooper to find him this morning."

"How did I know you were going to find some way to put Cooper into this?"

"I didn't put him there, Paloma Verdes did."

~ ~ ~

47

Mike pulled up in front of Giselle's place on Dana Point. There were no vehicles present. So where the fuck were they? He didn't like it. He opened the car door and pulled out his gun. The stupid bitch shouldn't have fucked him over. If she hadn't done that, he might well have let her live.

A light breeze was blowing in off the ocean. Mike ignored it as he approached the house. He tried the front door, and the knob turned easily under his hand. The house was empty. That was obvious within a few seconds. So where the hell had they gone?

Giselle wasn't that fucking smart. Mike knew it. So where the fuck had she gone? Was the kid smarter than they had anticipated? That was certainly possible. He had a hard time imagining it, given what he knew of the kid's sister, but then anything was possible.

Mike sighed. He wished that he knew what the fuck was going on. Except Vinnie Calabresi played his cards close to the damn chest. Calabresi was a big hitter in the California Mob. Big enough that he made Mike nervous, and Mike wasn't a man who got nervous easily.

Chapter Seven

Cooper had put both of them into the Eclipse along with the package. He wasn't sure where they were going to go at the moment, but away from here was the best answer that he could come up with. Women had gotten poor Rico into the middle of a Mob War and they were going to get the kid killed if Cooper couldn't come up with a way to solve his problem while keeping him alive.

He headed the car north towards Los Angeles. It was an hour away, but it would give them more room to hide than San Clemente had to offer. He looked in the mirror at Giselle. "You still haven't told us where you met Mike," Cooper reminded her...

"Tell him, Giselle, or I swear to God, I'll have him pull over and leave your sorry ass on the side of the road," Rico told her.

"Next stop coming up in fifty to seventy feet," Cooper said, applying his foot to the brake.

"Okay!" Giselle snapped, hugging herself.

"So start talking," Cooper told her.

"I met him in a club in San Diego. He was good looking and was flashing a lot of money around," Giselle shrugged, popping the piece of gum in her mouth. "We had a good time and then he said he had a job for me."

"What was the job?" Cooper asked. He was pretty sure that he knew already, but it would be best if Rico heard it from her.

"I was supposed to get close to Rico and wait."

"Why?"

"Mike told me that soon Rico would have a special delivery for Calabresi. I was supposed to snatch it and give it to Mike," Giselle said, hanging her head.

"So why didn't you?" Rico asked her, his voice as chilly as an ice berg in the north Atlantic.

"Because I like you," Giselle said softly.

"Oh, you like me? And that's why you got me fired and ripped me off? You have a fucking funny way of showing it," Rico threw his hands up in the air.

"Dammit Rico, I love you! That's why I didn't give Mike the real package," Giselle sobbed.

"You mean that?" Rico looked at her.

"I do, Rico," Giselle looked at him through tears. Cooper rolled his eyes. He understood, however. He had seen it before.

"Let's find a place to stay for the night and then we can talk this out," Cooper told them.

"That sounds like a plan," Rico said as he eyed Giselle.

~ ~ ~

Paloma Verdes looked around as she dialed Rico's cell phone. She had to let him know that Julian was pissed at him for not delivering the package to Calabresi. She was worried that Julian would kill Rico outright for stealing from him, even if Rico didn't realize it!

She was surprised when he actually answered his phone! "Rico, where have you been?" Paloma demanded.

"Around, Paloma. Stop giving me so much shit," Rico told her.

"Do you have any idea how much trouble you are in

right now? Julian has sent men out to find you!"

"And whose fault is that Paloma? I didn't ask for you to set me up as a mule for Mr. DiGeorgio," Rico yelled into the phone at her.

"I was trying to give us a better life, Enrico! I was trying to take care of you," Paloma sobbed.

"You were trying to get Mr. DiGeorgio to marry you, Paloma. I was just a step on the ladder, something that you could use to get closer to him."

"You are wrong, Enrico. I was trying to do the best I could for the both of us, to set us both up for life."

"I guess that makes it easier for you to sleep at night, telling yourself that," Rico shook his head.

"No, my brother, it is the truth!" Paloma almost whispered.

"If I survive this, Paloma, I never want to see you again! Do you understand me? Never again!" Rico broke the connection. He looked at Cooper. "DiGeorgio has men out looking for me."

"We knew that already. Right now, we need to get some rest and figure out a way to get them off your ass," Cooper replied.

"Did what you told your sister apply to me as well?" Giselle asked quietly from the back seat.

"That depends on you," Rico told her.

~ ~ ~

"Julian," Paloma said as she walked into DiGeorgio's office. DiGeorgio looked up at her, frowning.

"What is it?" he asked, leaning back in his chair.

"I have lost my brother. Rico doesn't love me anymore," Paloma said softly, tears running down her cheeks.

"He is a man, and he makes his own choices," DiGeorgio shrugged.

"You do not understand, Julian. He told me that he never wants to see me again!"

"Your brother, he no longer feels like he needs you. So you must forget him, Paloma. He has dismissed you, and you must dismiss him from your life. Otherwise, I will not be able to protect you," Julian said.

"Why would you need to protect me?" Paloma asked him, shocked.

"Because Calabresi is not a forgiving man. If you leave me, or try to help your brother, he will kill you and I will not be able to prevent it. I care deeply for you Paloma. You know this. But I will not throw away my life for you," DiGeorgio told her

"I know that, Julian," Paloma whispered softly.

"Make sure you do," Julian told her.

"So where are we headed," Renee Phillips asked. Gabriel King didn't answer as he pulled out of the Navy Yard.

"North," King told her.

"How far north?" Phillips asked.

"San Clemente," King replied.

"Why there?"

"Because that was the last place that Enrico Verdes was seen as he made some late deliveries today," King announced.

"You are positive of that?"

"I am. I have video confirmation."

"How? Did you get a signed warrant to get video of

Enrico Verdes?"

"Just get with the program, Phillips. Take my word for it," King sighed.

"Dammit, King, if you are breaking the law, I will have to arrest you," Phillips told him.

"You can try," King snorted.

"No King, I will do so. You seem to forget that you are supposed to uphold the laws of the United States," Phillips told him.

~ ~ ~

Cooper found a small roadside motel on the outskirts of Los Angeles. It was in one of the unincorporated zones, which made it a jurisdictional nightmare as far as police involvement was concerned. Cooper was okay with that. He paid for one room with two king-sized beds. Rico and Giselle had one and he took the one closest to the door.

For the moment, they were safe. At least for the night. Tomorrow, they would head back south to San Diego. Things would get tougher then. Cooper was trying to figure a way to deliver Calabresi's package on the way south without getting their head's blown off!

~ ~ ~

Giselle lay looking into darkness. She had fallen in love with Rico, and that went beyond saying. Except now, she had no idea if Rico still loved her. She hoped that he did, maybe even prayed that he did. However, she had no way of knowing for sure. Not unless he told her. And she was afraid to ask. She was afraid that she was going to be murdered by Mike, or some of his people. She feared for Rico as well. Cooper had said that he would help them, but she wasn't sure how much she believed him.

"What are you thinking about?" Rico whispered in her ear.

"I am worrying about our future," Giselle whispered back, turning over to face him.

"You aren't the only one. You have gotten us into a real mess, Babe.

"I am well aware of that. I think that maybe we will end up dead."

"I think Mr. Cooper will help us. He looks like he can handle himself," Rico assured her.

"I hope so," Giselle sighed, drawing comfort from the strength of his arms around her. Finally, they drifted off to sleep.

~ ~ ~

Phillips frowned every time she looked at Special Agent King of the Naval Criminal Investigative Services. He was off on one of his crusades, one that involved Mitch Cooper at least on a peripheral level. At the moment, it seemed to involve Cooper's client more than it did Cooper. But Phillips had a feeling that King was more concerned about Cooper's involvement.

Renee liked Cooper. He was an okay guy from what she had gotten to know of him. Cooper was a straight shooter, she liked that about him. He was a man who would do what he said he would do. A man of his word. That was a rare thing these days.

King was still a puzzle to her. It was obvious that there was bad blood between the two men. Sure, she knew what it was about, but not everybody did. King had finally told her the story, though he hadn't wanted to. By the time they got to San Clemente, the store that Enrico Verdes had made the delivery to was closed. Cursing, King drove into town to find them a motel for the night.

~ ~ ~

Morning. Cooper was the first one awake. He brewed coffee in the small room coffee maker. He was on his second cup and was brewing more when the two young people woke up. He had been thinking about his course of action for the day. First, he needed to make sure that Vinnie Calabresi got his package. That would get Calabresi off of their backs. Then he would have to find a way to make Mike and DiGeorgio back off. That might be a little bit harder.

Enrico was the first to roll out of bed and stumble to the bathroom. Cooper had a cup of coffee poured for him before he came out. "Thanks," Rico told him as he put a couple of packets of sugar and some creamer into it and then stirred it. He took a sip and sighed softly. "Good stuff," he said.

"It's not bad for motel coffee," Cooper said.

"No it isn't. I've drank a lot of motel coffee," Rico said.

"How much do you trust her?" Cooper asked, looking over at Giselle.

"I'm not sure," Rico admitted.

"How much do you trust your sister?"

"I don't," Rico told him.

"Not even a little?" Cooper asked.

"My sister looks out only for herself. She pays a lot of lip-service to taking care of family, but she comes first. How much do you trust my sister?" Rico asked, looking him in the eye.

"About as far as I can throw an elephant," Cooper told him.

"Then I guess we are on the same page. Paloma hired

you to find me, just so she could tell Julian DiGeorgio where I was. The fact that he will kill me on sight was secondary. By now, he has told her to cut her losses, or which I am one. Paloma would do so without a second thought," Enrico told him.

"That seems pretty harsh."

"It is. But it is also true."

"Would it upset you know that I have the same impression of her?"

"Not at all."

"I am going to try and help you, Rico. Giselle too if you think she is worth it," Cooper told him.

"I think she can be," Rico told him.

"I hope you are right."

"I am staking my life on it."

"Yes, you are," Cooper told him.

"You two do know I am awake?" Giselle asked as she sat up on the bed.

"We do now," Cooper told her.

"I would hope so. Mike will be coming after us," she said.

"In Los Angeles?" Cooper asked.

"Anywhere in Southern California," Giselle said.

"You know this how?" Cooper asked.

Chapter Eight

Mike Genovese frowned at Lucas Salvador as he walked into the room. "Where are they?" Genovese asked.

"We lost them. A couple of boys had the kid heading to a warehouse on Dana Point, but then we lost contact. The reason we lost contact is that both of the boys are dead. Seems like their car got blown up," Salvador shrugged.

"The kid has balls, I'll give him that. DeGrassi said the kid made all of his deliveries except for two, apologized for being late," Genovese shook his head.

"He let Mr. DiGeorgio know that?" Salvador asked.

"Sure, how else would I know?"

"Good point," Salvador nodded.

"Yeah, it is. Anyway, I want you to personally take the replacement package up to Mr. Calabresi. Mr. DiGeorgio says to take Carmine and Sally with you as protection. He also said to tell you not to fuck it up," Genovese told him.

"The package being put together in the usual place?"

"It is. Got call Carmine and Sally, tell them I said they are to stick to you like a sweaty shirt."

"Sure thing, Mike," Salvador nodded before turning and leaving the room. Mike Genovese watched him go. Genovese shook his head. He had tried to tell the boss that the Verdes woman was nothing but trouble. He had seen her kind before. Still, she had the boss under her spell. He walked back to his desk to call Falcone to let him know that Salvador would be personally delivering the package for Mr.

Calabresi.

~ ~ ~

Cooper left the two kids in the motel with a warning not to open the door for anyone, while he went to renew an old acquaintance with an L.A.P.D. cop named Hamilton. Dan Hamilton was one of the new breed of cops that looked like a soldier and had the same hungry look as a Doberman eyeing a steak. Cooper had met him working a case for the Office of Naval Intelligence back in the day.

"Been a long time, Cooper," Hamilton said as they shook hands. "Have a seat and let's catch up." Cooper took the seat across from Hamilton. Today, Hamilton was wearing a white short-sleeved dress shirt, charcoal gray slacks and a thin black tie. A suit jacket that matched the pants hung from a rack in the corner. His badge was clipped to his belt just in front of where his gun was holstered. "I heard you went private when you left the navy."

"You heard right. What do you know about a mob guy named Vinnie Calabresi?" Cooper asked.

"You never did like making small talk. But are you sure you want to tackle somebody of Calabresi's stature?" Hamilton looked a little stunned.

"I don't want to tackle him. I've got a kid that was set up to deliver some goods to him and then got ripped off by a girlfriend before he made the delivery. I'm trying to keep the kid alive."

"That's going to be a job. Who was the kid making the delivery for?"

"Julian DiGeorgio. And there is also some guy named Mike involved, he got the girlfriend to set the kid up."

"Mike? You got a last name to go with that?"

"The girl didn't catch it. They met in a club."

"Figures. You don't want much, do you Cooper?"

"Hey, I'm just trying to help keep the kid alive."

"Rico, are you sure you can trust this guy Cooper? You just met him last night," Giselle said.

"Yes, I trust him. Right now I trust him a lot more than I do you," Rico told her.

"That's a helluva thing to say to me!"

"You were the one that got the fucking Mob after us! If I had made my deliveries instead of running off with you, I wouldn't be knee deep in shit right now!"

"Do you want me to leave?" she asked defiantly.

"I don't, but if you want me to trust you again, you'll damn well have to earn it!" Rico snapped back at her.

"So how can I do that?"

"You can start by telling me everything you know about this Mike guy."

"Okay," Giselle sighed.

~ ~ ~

"Eddie, where the hell is my shipment?" Vinnie Calabresi asked as his head enforcer entered the room.

"I've got boys out looking, Boss," Falcone replied, trying to gauge his Boss's mood.

"I got a call from Deej's boy Genovese. He said that he's sending Lucas Salvador with a replacement package and he will be here by noon. You have until noon to find the original package, Eddie. Any later than that, I'm going to have to start wondering about you," Calabresi said.

"I'll have it for you, Mr. Calabresi," Eddie Falcone told him.

"I hope so," Calabresi said. Eddie Falcone headed for the door, a cold feeling in the pit of his stomach. There were few men who frightened him, but Vinnie Calabresi was one of them.

~ ~ ~

Mike groaned when he heard his cell phone ringing. He opened his eyes and rolled to a sitting position on the edge of his bed. He picked up his phone and looked at the screen and groaned again. He answered the call, "Detective Gordon," he announced.

"Hey Mike, the Chief wants your ass in at headquarters like an hour ago. There's a couple of fucking Navy cops here, and they want to talk to you," Sgt. Dennis Frame announced.

"Tell them half an hour," Mike said before hanging up. He put his phone down and headed for the shower. He had a pretty good idea why the Navy cops were here. They wanted the fucking kid, and right now, Mike Gordon had no goddamned idea of where the punk was at!

Twenty minutes later, Detective Mike Gordon was dressed and heading out the door of his one story walk-up apartment and down to his car. He'd stop at a Starbucks and grab a coffee on the way in. Chief Milton was not one of Mike Gordon's biggest fans. Though he knew that Gordon had the highest closure rate of any of the detectives on the San Clemente police department.

~ ~ ~

Chief Edward Milton was an imposing man. He stood nearly six foot six, was black as coal, and had a gleaming bald head. He towered over King, and Phillips was glad to see that he made her boss just a little uncomfortable. While

Camp Pendleton was a Marine base that bordered San Clemente, Milton was clearly no stranger to dealing with NCIS or people like Gabriel King. So Renee wisely leaned back in her chair and kept her mouth shut as King tried to explain why they were in Milton's town.

"Agent King, you say you are tracking a shipment of narcotics, but I have yet to hear anything approaching proof of that coming out of your mouth," Milton glared down at King, even though both men were sitting. Milton still towered more than a head above King.

"Chief Milton, we got a tip down in San Diego that said that a driver for Hi-Speed Deliveries was carrying a box of drugs from Julian DiGeorgio to Vincent Calabresi. We were told that the shipment was side-tracked," King explained.

"Who was the tip from?" Milton wanted to know.

"We have an undercover agent in DiGeorgio's operation. If he gets exposed, he is dead."

"I'm not asking for his name. I just want to know if he can be trusted," Milton leaned back in his chair and made a pyramid with his hands. He looked through it at King.

"'He can be trusted," King said.

"Detective Mike Gordon is my mob expert. He's been on Vinnie Calabresi for a few years. If Calabresi is involved, Gordon will know it," Milton said.

"I hope you're right. I hope he is clean," King nodded.

"I do too," Milton said.'

"What exactly do you mean by that?" Renee Phillips asked.

""Most of the cases against Calabresi and his men have gone south over the past year. Mike Gordon was the man in charge of those investigations. I have my suspicions, but if

I were to assign somebody to look at him from within my department, Gordon would know. You guys are actually a blessing in disguise," Milton shrugged.

"Wow, and you can say that with a straight face?" King asked, looking incredulous.

"I can. Sometimes, you need an outsider to clean out the sewers, King."

"I guess I understand that," King nodded.

"I hope so," Milton told him. Renee Phillips rolled her eyes. Why the fuck couldn't the two men just ask each other for help? Was it really all that hard?

"I can't believe you two," she said, shaking her head. Both of them looked at her. "Why the hell is it so hard for men to ask each other for help?

~ ~ ~

Mitch Cooper pulled into the hotel after his chat with Dan Hamilton. He hoped that the kids would still be in the room. He felt like the boy would, but the girl he was uncertain about. She was the wildcard in the deck. Cooper climbed out of his car and headed for the room. He unlocked the door and stepped inside, happy to see that the pair were still there, waiting on him. He also noticed that Giselle didn't look any too happy about it.

"Glad you decided to stay," Cooper told them.

"Not like we had a choice," Giselle said, archly.

"Giselle there is always a choice. You are free to walk out that door at any time. The thing is, if you do, you will take full responsibility for whatever happens to you. You leave I will not protect you. That is your choice. So what's it going to be?" Cooper asked.

"When you put it that way, I guess I'm going to stay. I'd

stay for Rico anyway," Giselle said.

"Rico, what about you?" Cooper looked at him.

"I decided to stick with you last night. You saw those guys coming after me. You helped me get away. I owe you my life," Rico replied.

"Good then we all know where we stand," Cooper said.

"And, Giselle told me more about this Mike guy. It seems he's a cop in San Clemente," Rico explained.

"It would have been helpful to know that information last night," Cooper glared at her.

"It didn't seem relevant, you talking about the Mob and all," Giselle shrugged.

"Anything to do with Rico and that package is relevant," Cooper told her. "Why would a cop want you to steal it?"

"How the fuck should I know? I ain't his squeeze," Giselle snarled, sparks shooting from her eyes.

"It matters to Rico, because his life is the one on the line. If you really care for him as much as you claim, it should be important to you."

"Fuck you, Cooper."

"Not with a ten-foot fucking pole, Giselle. I've seen your type before. You snuggle up to guys, get them in trouble, and then cut and run at the first sign of trouble. Like I said, you are more than welcome to walk out that door right now," Cooper told her.

"You'd be happy if I did, wouldn't you?" Giselle yelled.

"I could care less one way or the other. My only concern is keeping Rico alive," Cooper told her.

"Giselle, shut the fuck up! I've had enough of your goddamn attitude! If you aren't willing to do what I say, then you better walk out that goddamn door right now,"

Rico yelled at her. Giselle flinched and blinked away tears. This wasn't the Rico she had wrapped around her little finger, and she wasn't sure that she liked seeing this side of him.

"Baby," she started.

"Shut up. If you aren't with me and Cooper, then you are against us. And if you are against us, you best get out of here right now!"

"I'm with you Rico. I done told you that I love you," Giselle whispered contritely.

Chapter Nine

San Clemente, California.

San Clemente was built by Ole Hanson and he called it the Spanish Village by the Sea. Cooper remembered reading that somewhere. He would need to check a telephone directory, something that was fading fast in this age of internet and virtual address books. The police station was still located on the Presidio.

Gordon pulled into the parking lot and climbed out of his car. He was wondering why Chief Milton was wanting to see him, and also what the hell that the NCIS agents wanted. Sure, Camp Pendleton was on the other side of the highway, but what did that have to do with him? There was no way that anybody could have found out about his deal with Falcone. They had both been too careful to make sure that their meets went unobserved and completely off the books. So what the fuck was going on?

There was only one way to find out, so he guessed that he had better get to it. Mike Gordon pushed open the door and entered the station. He headed for the elevator that would take him to the Chief's office. He would just have to take this bull by the horns and hope he didn't get gored.

~ ~ ~

Vinnie Calabresi watched Fast Eddie Falcone climb into his car and leave. He looked at Marco Gratziono. "Follow Eddie and let me know where he goes and who he talks to. Everyone, understand?"

"Yes Boss," Gratziono replied as he exited the room. Calabresi took a seat behind his desk. He removed a cigar from the humidor, bit off the end and spat it into the waste basket and then put it in his mouth and lit it. Eddie was getting a little big for his britches of late.

Eddie was getting cocky, acting just a little too sure of himself. That was usually the mark of a man getting ready to attempt a coup, one that would raise his own status at the expense of the boss that he served. Calabresi had been there, had done it himself. That was one of the reasons he kept an eye out for it.

Eddie had his eye on Julian DiGeorgio's territory. But Deej was a competent underboss, and his peace offering was a sincere effort to keep the peace. So why was Eddie so ready to pounce on Julian? He wondered if maybe Eddie had something to do with the original shipment going missing. If that was the case, Fast Eddie would have to put the brakes on the replacement shipment that Deej had promised to send.

Vinnie Calabresi reached for his phone. He punched in Julian's number. He listened to it ring. DiGeorgio answered on the second ring. "Julian, who have you got bringing me the replacement shipment?" he asked.

"Lucas Salvador, Carmine Infantino, and Sully Carboza," Julian DiGeorgio answered.

"Call them and tell them to be extra careful and not to trust Fast Eddie if he should try to stop them. I'm thinking Fast Eddie maybe trying for a coup," Calabresi told him.

"I'll call them and let them know as soon as we are done talking, Mr. Calabresi," DiGeorgio told him.

"Good. Something smells, Deej. I am afraid that I have

a rat in my crew. If you hear anything, you will let me know?"

"On my mother's grave," DiGeorgio replied.

"Thank you," Calabresi told him, meaning it. He hung up, and he knew that DiGeorgio was already calling his men to pass the warning along.

"I have an idea," Mitch Cooper told the kids in the room with him. He had been thinking of the best way to broach the subject.

"I'm all ears, Mr. Cooper. I don't want to die," Rico said softly. Giselle wisely kept her mouth shut. She could tell she was on very thin ice with both men.

"I'm going to call Calabresi and set up a meet to deliver the package," Cooper told them.

"Are you out of your fucking mind?" Giselle exploded, sitting up.

"Do you have a better idea?" Cooper looked at her.

"Sure, just go ahead and put a gun to our heads and pull the trigger," Giselle huffed.

"Tell me your plan," Rico said, shooting Giselle a dirty look.

"Rico are you fucking nuts? This man is gonna get us both killed!" Giselle exclaimed, jumping to her feet.

"You know where the door is!" Rico snapped at her. Giselle flinched as if he had slapped her. She sure as hell didn't like this side of him!

"If we can get Calabresi the package, it takes some of the heat off Rico. That only leaves your friend Mike and whoever the hell he is working for," Cooper told her.

"Mike is gonna fuck you both seven ways to Sunday," Giselle shook her head.

"Mike is your problem, Giselle," Cooper told her.

"How you figure that?" Giselle asked.

"He hired you to steal the package and you already double-crossed him once. You think he is going to believe a word out of your mouth after that?" Cooper asked.

"Probably not," Giselle admitted.

"Then you walk out that door and start running now, or you take your chances with us and maybe get out of this alive."

"You are one hard ass sonofabitch!"

"That's why I make the big bucks. So what is it going to be Giselle? Are you with us or against us?" Cooper asked, his eyes locked on hers.

"I guess I'm in. Don't seem like I got a choice."

"You always have a choice. We are just the better one."

~ ~ ~

"We need to ignore Fast Eddie if he tries to contact us," Carmine told Salvador.

"Why is that?" Salvador asked.

"Orders from the Boss. Seems that Fast Eddie Falcone is suspected of being a rat," Carmine explained.

"Got it," Lucas nodded.

"Vinnie thinks that Eddie is a rat for the Feds."

"So if he gets in touch, we fucking shoot on sight," Carmine nodded.

"That sounds like a plan," Lucas agreed.

"It sounds like a good one," Carmine noted.

~ ~ ~

"We've all heard that line, "Uneasy lies the head that wears the crown." It is never truer than when it applies to the leadership of organized crime families. Because there is always some younger guy that wants to take their place, some up and comer who thinks they can do it better, make things run smoother, make a better profit. Fast Eddie Falcone was one of those type.

"The thing is, Fast Eddie was nothing more than an enforcer, and he never would ever be more than that. Sure, he was slick and creative, but he had no sense of finesse. He didn't think I would see what he was up to, but Eddie was wrong," Vinnie Calabresi explained to Joe "The Monster" Gambino.

"Falcone has been trying to throw his weight around lately. You think he's in the Fed's pocket?" Gambino asked.

"If he ain't, he soon will be. Joe, I'm giving you the paper on Fast Eddie Falcone. He needs to be put down like a rabid dog before he hurts Our Thing. I want to be able to light a candle for him when I go to mass tomorrow," Calabresi ordered.

"I'll take Leo and Dominic with me. We should have his head in a bag by sunset," Joe told him.

"Thank you Joe, for taking care of this for me. Do this and I'm putting you in charge of my personal security," Vinnie said.

"Consider it done, Boss," Joe said before turning and walking out of Calabresi's office. Vinnie Calabresi leaned back in his chair and fired up a fat cigar. He had called Julian and had him warn his delivery team about Eddie. Sending Joe after the greedy sonofabitch was just insurance in case Deej's boys couldn't handle him. His phone started ringing and he snatched it up. "Yeah?"

"Mr. Calabresi, I have a package that belongs to you and I want to make sure it gets to you. The delivery was supposed to happen a couple of days ago but got delayed," Mitch Cooper said. He had gone and bought a burner phone to make this call with, because he wasn't about to take a chance on Calabresi learning his real name.

"Do you now?" Calabresi asked, his voice as smooth as snake oil.

"The delivery guy had his head turned by a girl who was acting under the orders of a guy named Mike. I was hired to find the delivery guy and keep him alive. I figure the best way to do that is to make sure you got your package."

"That will get me off his ass, but I'm not so sure about the sender. He was so upset, he sent me a replacement package and ate the cost as part of doing business," Calabresi replied.

"I was hoping you could intercede on the kid's behalf. He's a good kid, but he didn't stand a chance against the temptress that was sent after him."

"A man needs to think with his big head, not the one between his legs," Calabresi told him.

"I agree, but when you are young, dumb, and full of cum, what can you be expected to do? You remember what it was like being young, don't you Mr. Calabresi?" Cooper asked.

"Yeah I do. I'll talk to the sender but I make no promises. Where do you want to deliver my package?"

"How about I drop it off at Fratellos Italian Restaurant with the manager? You don't have to pick it up in person. I hope you will call me and let me know when you have it. Strictly as a courtesy."

"You have a deal. Fifteen minutes, my boys will be there to pick it up. If it is the right package, I'll try to help your boy out. If it's not, or if the cops show up, all bets are off," Calabresi said.

"It will be there," Cooper told him and then broke the connection. He pulled the battery out of the burn phone and laid it on the seat. He carried the package in and left it with the manager and then headed back towards the car. Rico and Giselle both looked anxious.

"Now what?" Rico asked as Copper climbed back in the car.

"Now we wait," Cooper told them. He pulled out of the parking lot and drove down a couple of lots and pulled in where he could keep an eye on the front of Fratellos.

Surveillance, by definition, sucks. It involves a lot of sitting and waiting for something to happen. With luck, this surveillance wouldn't take too long. The clock was ticking and Cooper wanted to make sure that Calabresi's men picked up the package. He knew that they would take it back out to the car before they opened it to confirm its contents. Cooper had done the same thing to make sure that Giselle wasn't fucking Rico over a second time. He figured that Calabresi could call DiGeorgio off from killing Rico.

Ten minutes had passed when he watched Calabresi's men pull into the lot and enter the restaurant. He had given the manager a hundred dollar bill to make sure he gave it to the right men. He watched through binoculars, filming as he did so as they carried the box to their car. Five more minutes passed before the car pulled out of the lot. Cooper put the battery back in the burn phone and headed south, back to San Diego. He figured it wouldn't take long for Calabresi to call him back.

He was right. Three minutes later, the phone rang. He

accepted the call. "Did you get it?" he asked.

"I did," Calabresi answered.

"Will you make that call and try to square things for the kid?" Cooper asked.

"I am a man of my word. But tell your client to be more careful where he sticks his dick in the future," Calabresi told him. Cooper broke the connection without saying good-bye, and tossed the phone out the window, watching it shatter as it hit the pavement at 60 miles per hour.

"Calabresi is off your back for now. However, we've still got to deal with Julian DiGeorgio. He may be a bit harder," Cooper told the kid.

Chapter Ten

"Hey, Chief, I understand that you wanted to see me?" Mike Gordon asked as he entered the Chief's office. He pretended not to notice the man and woman, but he was pretty sure that they were the Feds he had been warned about.

"Have a seat, Gordon,' Chief Milton commanded. Gordon did, glancing once more at the two Feds. He didn't like the looks of the man at all, but the woman was easy on the eyes.

"These are Agents King and Phillips from NCIS. They are here to ask you about the local drug trade," Milton explained.

"So what do you want to know?" Gordon asked, putting on his best poker face.

"Who runs the local drug trade up here? Seems like we've had more than a few Marines overdosing on base," King said, using the story that he, Phillips and Chief Milton had agreed upon. There had been some overdoses on the base but not nearly as many as King was suggesting.

"Anything illegal would be coming through one of two people, either Vincent Calabresi or one of his top men, a guy named Eddie Falcone," Gordon said in a bored tone.

"Tell us about Falcone," King suggested.

"Fast Eddie Falcone, he's a New York transplant that came out here to work for Vincent Calabresi about ten years ago. He's reputed to be Calabresi's top enforcer, but it's getting around that Fast Eddie is no longer happy with his position and is looking to move up the corporate ladder.

"He's been trying to move in south of here on territory under Julian DiGeorgio's control and DiGeorgio has been pushing back. It's been causing some bad blood between Calabresi and DiGeorgio," Gordon shrugged.

"Could Falcone be behind the disappearance of a delivery truck that was rumored to be carrying a special package to Calabresi from DiGeorgio?" King asked, watching Gordon's face very closely.

"I wouldn't know," Gordon replied, trying to keep the shock off his face. How the hell did they know? He was sure that nobody but he and Eddie knew that they had arranged for it to happen! Had the fucking kid gone to the cops? His heart was racing and he forced himself to breathe normally.

"Is that a fact?" King looked intense. Gordon could feel the sweat starting to bead out on his forehead.

"That's what I said," Gordon shrugged.

"Then why do we have pictures of you meeting with Falcone at Dana Point?" King asked. Gordon's face blanched, losing all color. He was sweating freely now.

"Where is Falcone, Gordon?" Chief Milton asked. Milton looked like a storm cloud getting ready to break and unleash a torrential downpour.

"I have no fucking idea, Chief!" Gordon snapped back angrily.

"Bullshit, Mike. I've been hearing whispers for months about you being dirty. Hell, none of Calabresi's people have so much as a traffic ticket since you've been in OCB. It didn't take a lot to figure out why. And, you just confirmed it," Milton told him.

"That's bullshit, Chief, and you know it!"

"No, Mike it isn't. IA has had you under discreet surveillance for a couple of months now. I'm gonna ask you to come clean now and save yourself the embarrassment of being perp-walked in front of the press," Milton told him.

"Well shit," Mike Gordon sighed.

~ ~ ~

"Where are we going now?" Rico asked.

"To get your truck so you can take it back. I figure that will buy you a little with both DeGrassi and DiGeorgio. I'm sure that Calabresi has already let DiGeorgio know that he received the original package, and will keep the back-up and the money as reparation for the delivery being late. However, if you take the truck back, it could buy you a little slack while I figure out how to get you off the hook with DiGeorgio," Cooper replied.

"You think Rico is going to be stupid enough to go back?" Giselle asked in astonishment from behind them.

"I think it might be the safest thing that he could do," Cooper replied quietly.

"Rico, baby, if you go back, DiGeorgio is gonna have your Mexican ass drawn and fucking quartered!" Giselle exploded.

"Maybe not. Mr. DiGeorgio understands respect and acting like a man," Rico said, thoughtfully.

"Rico are you trying to commit suicide?" Giselle looked at him like he was crazy. She was sure that he had to have lost his mind.

"Giselle, before you say another fucking word, I want you to remember that you are the one that got me into all of this trouble to begin with!" Rico snapped.

"Me?" she sounded stunned.

"Yes, goddamn it, *you*! You were the one that talked me into taking off with all of those packages still left to deliver. I should have tossed your ass out of the truck. I was thinking with my dick and not with my brain. That isn't the case anymore. You'll do what I say or we can stop and let your ass out on the side of the road! If you really loved me, you'd be trying to help me get out of this instead of trying to get me in a worse situation," Rico told her.

"I can't believe you're treating me this way!" Giselle yelled at him. Cooper swung the Eclipse to the side of the highway. Rico opened the door and climbed out, pulling the passenger seat forward so she could get out of the back seat.

"Get out, Giselle. I'm done with you," Rico told her. Her gaze hardened as she glared at him.

"You are making a damn big mistake, Rico. You don't know how big, but you will. And when you are screaming as you watch your guts tumbling out of your belly onto the floor, you remember I told you so!" Giselle snarled as she climbed out of the car. Rico pushed the seat back and got in. He shut the door and Cooper put the car in drive and pulled away, leaving the girl standing there on the side of the road.

"That was rough," Rico sighed, closing his eyes as they drove towards the warehouse.

"Nobody has ever said doing the right thing was easy," Cooper told him.

"No they didn't. I liked Giselle a lot. She didn't love me. Not like she said any way."

"It is a rare thing to find real love, Rico. Most of us settle, because we find somebody that we are just comfortable with. To find love, true love, that is a lot harder," Cooper told him.

"What is real love?" Rico asked.

"I'm not sure that there is a real definition for it. However, to me, real love is something ethereal. It is an indefinable quality. Love is more than sex. Love is an emotional attachment, a bit of pure soul to soul communication. It's a cosmic connection that goes beyond the physical attraction and into something far more intimate. While what you had with Giselle was nice, and I am sure physically pleasing, her soul wasn't in it. And if you are honest with yourself, neither was yours," Cooper replied.

"That makes sense," Rico nodded.

"I'm glad," Cooper nodded.

~ ~ ~

Giselle watched them drive away and then threw back her head and screamed as loudly as she could! She couldn't believe it! Rico had literally just thrown her to the curb! She pulled out her cell phone. She hadn't thrown it away like that Cooper guy had told her to. She dialed Mike's number. He would know what to do.

~ ~ ~

Mike Gordon's cell phone started ringing. He pulled it out and looked at the caller ID. It was Giselle. Fuck, talking to that bitch right now was the last fucking thing he needed to do, especially in front of the Chief and the two Navy cops. He hit the button to ignore and turned his phone off. He would call her back later if he wasn't under arrest himself.

"Who was that?" King asked him.

"Nobody I need to talk to right now," Gordon shrugged.

"How long have you been in bed with Calabresi, Mike?"

Chief Gordon asked sadly. It was obvious that he hated seeing one of his men go over to the dark side.

"Eddie Falcone approached me in The Red Fox Lounge over on El Camino Real. It was right after the Sanchez bust that went south on us and Mendez got killed. Falcone made all the right noises, asked me if I wanted to start making some real money and maybe avoiding getting shot down in the streets. I'd downed about three doubles of good bourbon, and it sounded pretty damn good. All I had to do was start looking the other way when Calabresi's men were making deals, and he'd feed me names of the competition so I could keep up on my arrests," Gordon sighed.

"So how much were you making from Calabresi?"

"Enough that I could be fired today and not have to worry about it," Gordon admitted.

"Put your gun and badge on the desk, Gordon. You are suspended, pending a full investigation. Without pay," Milton told him, his face looking like it had been carved from granite.

"I already figured that was coming. Chief, you aren't never gonna stop these guys. For every one that you take down, five more are going to pop up to take their place. As long as people want the dope, they are gonna be around to sell it. The war on drugs has been about as effective as Prohibition was," Gordon said.

"Doesn't really fucking matter, Gordon. Right now, the law makes it illegal. We are in the legal and illegal business, not the right and wrong business. Get the fuck out of my sight!" Milton roared, his voice rising at the end.

Gordon stood and put his gun and badge on the desk, and then he turned and walked out of the Chief's office. He saw no reason to stop and talk to anyone on his way out. Once he was outside, he pulled his phone out and called Giselle. He wanted to get his hands on that stupid bitch and her fucking dumb-ass boyfriend!

~ ~ ~

"That could certainly have gone better," Renee Phillips said.

"Maybe, maybe not. He pretty much confessed to being dirty," King said.

"He was tricked into it," Milton pointed out.

"A confession is still a confession. And if you put IAD on him now, they can still prove it," King pointed out.

"I know that, but I still don't feel exactly comfortable about it," Milton sighed as he dropped into his chair.

"Every dirty cop that you get off the street makes things better for the good ones," Phillips pointed out.

"I know that too. The problem is, I liked that stupid fuck. I thought that he was one of the good ones."

"Bad cops are like chameleons, Chief. They hide in plain sight," King pointed out.

"That doesn't make it any easier," Milton sighed.

"What the fuck do you want Giselle? You guys fucking pulled a disappearing act on me!" Mike said when then girl answered the phone.

"I couldn't help that. Some fucking private eye that Rico's sister hired found us and talked him into going back after delivering the original package to Calabresi," Giselle said. The anger in her voice was evident, and Mike picked up on that.

"Then what?" he asked.

"Then that son of a bitch Rico had Cooper toss me out on the curb! Out on the fucking side of the fucking highway! I need a fucking ride, Mike!"

"Where are you at?" Mike asked, feeling like maybe he still had a chance to come out of the whole deal on top.

"I'm about five miles north of the warehouse. They said they was going to pick up the delivery van and take it back to DeGrassi," Giselle told him.

"I'll pick up in about twenty minutes, Giselle, and then we are going to go take care of Rico and that fucking private eye," Mike told her.

"I'll be watching for you," she told him.

"Do that," Gordon told her as he climbed into his car and hung up. Yeah, he'd pick Giselle up, but she wasn't going to survive too fucking long after he did. She was a fucking loose end and he didn't want Internal Affairs or the two Navy cops getting to her!

~ ~ ~

Fast Eddie Falcone sat parked on the side of the road. His engine was running, and he was alert, watching for a car that he knew would be coming up from San Diego. He knew who to look for. He was going to make sure that the second shipment never reached Calabresi either. That would make it easier when he made his move to push Julian DiGeorgio out of San Diego. He removed his pistol from the holster under his arm and checked it, making sure that the magazine was full and that there was one in the chamber. A full load. There was a loaded shotgun on the seat beside him. Fast Eddie felt like he was being held back because he had come out from the East Coast. These West Coast guys didn't trust him; they had made that pretty goddamn clear. He was going to have his due, one way or another!

Chapter Eleven

"I've got a bad feeling. Maybe we shouldn't have left Giselle like that," Rico said.

"Giselle is a survivor, Rico. You should know that by now," Cooper told him.

"I do, but I still feel bad about it."

"Anybody would, kid. That girl is nothing but bad news. I have a feeling she could make your sister look like a saint."

"Paloma is far from being a saint," Rico shook his head.

"I know," Cooper told him.

"Do you really think taking the truck back is a good move?"

"I do. We can time it so we can drop it off at night when nobody is there. I'll put you in a safe house while I negotiate with Julian DiGeorgio to keep you alive," Cooper told him.

"Do you think you can pull that off?" Rico looked at him, studying his face.

"If I didn't, I wouldn't have suggested it," Cooper told him.

"I get that. So what do you think is going on?"

"I think that a mob war is brewing, Rico. And I think that you might be right in the middle of it."

"Why me?" Rico asked.

"Maybe we should ask your sister about that," Cooper told him.

"Paloma! Why can she never leave me alone to live my own life?"

"She is your older sister. She feels like she has to watch over you. My sister was the same way," Cooper smiled, remembering.

"You have an older sister too?" Enrico asked.

"I did. She's gone now," Cooper replied, sadness creeping into his voice.

"I'm so sorry. Were you close?"

"We were. She took care of me when we were growing up. I admit, I adored her and would have done anything for her. I was on my first deployment when she died."

"Deployment?" Rico questioned.

"I was in the Navy, on a ship in the Persian Gulf when she died. I was on a mission with my team and out of contact. I didn't find out until a week after it had happened. She was driving home from work one night and got hit head on by a drunk driver. Both the drunk and she died instantly," Cooper said. "I missed the funeral too. So I never really got to say goodbye."

"You have my sympathy, Mr. Cooper. However you are right. Paloma drives me crazy most of the time, but she is my sister and I love her. I just can't stand her trying to manage my life," Rico sighed.

"We can't pick family, Rico. We just have to accept them for who they are. I don't think you would ever find what you were looking for with Giselle. She only cared about herself. Now your friend Lara, that girl cares about you. She was the one that warned me about DeGrassi being a mobster."

"Lara is a good girl. Paloma didn't like her because she wasn't wealthy and was just a regular person. To hear Paloma tell it, Lara wasn't good enough for me."

"What did you think?" Cooper asked.

"I think Lara was a great gal, but I don't know. We only went out the one time."

"She made enough of an impression that you wanted to tell Paloma about her."

"She did, and when I did, that turned into a bigger disaster than the Titanic."

"Love is never easy, Rico. That's what makes it worth fighting for."

"I'll have to think about that for a while."

Cooper pulled into the warehouse parking lot. It looked empty. He took that as a good sign. It suggested that none of DiGeorgio's men had found the place. Still, Cooper drew the Beretta as they approached the door. If there was somebody waiting inside, he wanted to be ready. He stood back a bit as Enrico opened the door, and then slipped inside ahead of him. The place was empty except for the truck. Cooper breathed a sigh of relief.

He holstered his weapon and then they gave the truck a good search to make sure that it hadn't been compromised. No bombs, always a good sign. "You start the truck and drive out. I'll follow you and keep off any predators," Cooper told him, turning and heading back to the Eclipse.

He heard the delivery van's engine start and Rico was driving out of the warehouse as he reached his car. Cooper got in and fired the engine and put the car in gear, sliding out of the parking lot and taking up a defensive position behind it as they headed back south towards San Diego.

~ ~ ~

"Get in," Mike told Giselle when he pulled up beside her. Giselle gave him a hard look before opening the door and climbing in. Mike had the car moving before she had her seatbelt fastened. "Where do you think they are headed?" he asked.

"Cooper had some crazy idea about taking the van back to DeGrassi. So they are probably going to the warehouse," Giselle replied, anger flaring in her eyes. Whatever she might have once felt for Rico had now been replaced by hate, and it was a hatred that burned as hot as the fires of hell!

"Then I guess we head for the warehouse," Mike said, stepping on the gas.

"Mike, if Rico has to die, I want to be the one that pulls the trigger on his sorry ass," Giselle said

"Sure thing," Mike told her.

"Thanks," Giselle breathed. Rico was going to pay for dumping her on the side of the road like garbage. So would Cooper.

Mike Gordon drove to the warehouse and pulled into the gravel parking lot. The lock was off the door. He heard Giselle muttering to herself as she climbed out and hit the button that would raise the door. The warehouse was empty. The truck was gone. Giselle screamed in rage. Gordon looked at her and smiled. The woman scorned. He almost felt sorry for the kid when they found him. Giselle would not make Rico's death a quick one. He could tell.

Eddie Falcone spotted the car that he had been looking for. He smiled, but it never reached his eyes. He stepped out of the car, drawing the shotgun out as he did. He worked the pump and lifted the gun, aiming at the rapidly approaching windshield. He fired. The one ounce slug punched a hole through the windshield and the driver's head. The car veered off the road and into a ditch, and then launched itself into the air. It landed on the roof and then burst into the flames. Fast Eddie smiled. He walked across the road and worked the slide again. He could see movement inside the car. At least one of DiGeorgio's men was still alive in there. Too bad for him. Eddie Falcone lifted the shotgun again and fired through the window. The man died.

Eddie didn't care who they were. He was here to send a message. But it wasn't just for Julian DiGeorgio. It was for Vinnie Calabresi as well. Eddie was going to take his place as crown prince. He didn't care if the old guard liked it or not!

There was a third man inside the car, but it appeared he had died on impact. Eddie broke out one of the side windows and extracted the replacement package and the money. Vinnie wasn't going to be happy when neither arrived as DiGeorgio had promised. Eddie grinned all the way back to his car. He tossed both the box with the dope and the briefcase with money in and climbed in behind it.

Eddie fired the engine and pulled onto the highway. He headed back towards San Diego. It was time to make Julian DiGeorgio jumpy. And he knew exactly how he was going to do it.

It was nearly ten p.m. when Rico pulled up in front of the Delivery Service offices. He locked the truck and dropped the key in through the mail slot. He looked at the door wistfully, before turning and climbing into the Eclipse with Cooper. Cooper put the car in gear and pulled out onto the street. "So what now?" Rico asked.

"I'm going to take you to one of my safe houses and then we are going to get a good night's sleep. In the morning, we will try to figure out how to get Julian DiGeorgio off your back," Cooper replied.

"Sounds like as good a plan as any," Rico sighed.

~ ~ ~

Twenty minutes later, they were in one of several safe houses that Cooper had located around the city. The safe houses were a hold-over from his days as a Navy spy. They had proven invaluable since he had turned private investigator, and he often used them to protect clients and witnesses. They had also had helped him to avoid cops and bad guys as well.

As both a Navy SEAL and an officer in Naval Intelligence, he had made a lot of enemies. As a private eye, he had added to the list. So having places to disappear to at a moment's notice had seemed like a good idea.

"You want a drink?" Cooper asked, turning on the television. The Padres were playing the Giants in the second half of a double header.

"I could go for a beer," Rico said as he looked around.

"Have a seat. Killian's Red okay? It's all I've got besides Jim Beam."

"Killian's is good. You really got a nice place here, Cooper."

"Thanks. I try to keep the place up," Cooper shrugged. He vanished into the kitchen and then emerged with two open bottles of Killian's Red. He handed one to Rico and took a seat.

"Am I going to die, Cooper?" Rico asked.

"Not if I can help it, Pal. You got caught up in a power

struggle, first between your sister and Giselle. And then between DiGeorgio and Calabresi. Then there is also this Mike guy and Eddie Falcone. We've got you squared away with Calabresi. Now we have to get DiGeorgio off your back," Cooper told him.

"Any ideas on that yet?"

"Maybe we can get your sister to help."

"Oh yeah, good luck with that!" Rico rolled his eyes and then took a long pull on the beer.

"Paloma may be the best chance you have, Rico. You told me that she's close to DiGeorgio."

"I did and she is. I don't know how close, or how pissed he may be at her for trying to help me," Rico shook his head.

"So in the morning, we call her and find out," Cooper told him.

"That's your plan?"

"It is for the moment. If we need to, we'll improvise."

"Improvise?"

"Yeah, you know, make it up as we go along."

"Right," Rico sighed.

~ ~ ~

"Why are you helping me, Mike?" Giselle asked, looking over at the man that had set her after Rico.

"Because Rico fucked us both, Kid. He needs to pay for that. Also, killing him removes one more witness against me for the cops." Mike shrugged,

"I thought you were a cop?"

"Were, is the operative word there. I got suspended today over this shit with Rico and Fast Eddie."

"That sucks."

"Yes it does. Still, it's all part of the game. We get Rico

and that Cooper guy, we might have a chance to survive this mess."

"Who is going to protect us if you ain't a cop no more?"

"Eddie Falcone. He's making a power grab. That's what all of this is about."

"A power grab?" Giselle looked at him, her brow wrinkled.

"Eddie is tired of being an enforcer. He wants a seat at the table of bosses," Gordon explained.

"Why do I get a feeling that we gonna get fucked?" Giselle asked.

"We won't. Eddie will take care of us," Gordon told her, hoping that he was right and that Eddie wouldn't fuck them over like he was Calabresi.

"You better be right," Giselle sighed.

Fast Eddie Falcone lay on a hillside behind Julian DiGeorgio's house. He lay prone on the ground behind a Remington 700 chambered for 7mm rounds. The lights were on all over the house down below. He could see the palace guard moving around the grounds, doing their security checks.

A fat lot of good that would do them in a few seconds. He could see Julian DiGeorgio through the patio doors. It would be so fucking easy to put a bullet through his head right now. Except that wouldn't get him what he wanted. No, he wanted the man running scared, wondering where the bullet would come from that ended him, but not knowing who had pulled the trigger. Maybe he could set up Mike Gordon for the hit. That would eliminate yet another problem. Eddie looked through the scope and centered his crosshairs on a man. He took a deep breath, let it halfway out as his finger slowly squeezed the trigger. The rifle bucked against his shoulder and a dead man dropped into the pool. Eddie worked the bolt and fired again.

Chapter Twelve

"What exactly did we do other than waste the day up in San Clemente?" Renee Phillips asked.

"We exposed a dirty cop, for one thing. We also got a lead on who was running most of the drugs in San Diego," Gabriel King told her.

"Julian DiGeorgio has been on the SDPD radar for a long time," Phillips pointed out.

"What about Fast Eddie Falcone?"

"Him, not so much. He was considered a low-level enforcer and not much else," Phillips sighed.

"What do you think about him now?"

"I think that maybe he deserves a closer look. It appears that none of us noticed how ambitious he was."

"Yeah, I kinda figured that out," Gabriel King rolled his eyes.

"So how do you think Mitch Cooper is involved?" Phillips asked, deciding to poke the bear.

"Who the fuck knows with Cooper? But I'm sure he is in it up to his asshole," King replied.

"So what are we going to do now?"

"Go home and get a good night's sleep. We'll tackle it fresh in the morning," King sighed.

"That actually sounds like the best idea you've had today," Phillips said.

~ ~ ~

Fast Eddie Falcone was chuckling to himself as he

drove away from DiGeorgio's house. He figured DiGeorgio had shit his pants when the bullets had started punching through the windows of his house and his men had started dying. Now he had to find a way to pin the shooting on Mike Gordon. He figured it wouldn't take too much for DiGeorgio to snap and lose it. When that happened, he would step in and take his place at the table with the rest of the bosses. He would take the place that he deserved!

Eddie pulled out his phone and dialed Mike Gordon's number. "Gordon," the man answered.

"It's Eddie. Did you get the package?" Falcone asked.

"Unfortunately, no. Some fucking private eye from San Diego rescued the kid and talked him into dumping Giselle on the side of the road. She didn't take kindly to that and wants to put a bullet into the kid and the private eye," Gordon replied.

"Where are you at?" Eddie asked.

"About fifteen minutes from San Diego."

"Then we should meet up," Eddie told him.

"When and where?" Gordon asked.

~ ~ ~

Mitch sat alone in the kitchen, a bottle of vodka on the table beside him, a cup filled with a combination of vodka and cranberry-grape juice in front of him. He picked it up and took a drink.

Tomorrow he would call Julian DiGeorgio and see if he couldn't bargain for Enrico Verdes' life. He had no idea if he would be successful or not, but he had to try. He took another drink from the glass. He pulled out his cell phone and dialed Renee Phillips' number. She answered on the first ring. "Hello?" she asked.

"Hello, Renee," Cooper said.

"Did you find the kid?" she asked.

"I did."

"How did that work out?"

"It was a bit on the rough side, but we managed."

"Glad to hear it. So why did you call?"

"I called to see how you were," Cooper told her.

"King wants a piece of your ass," Phillips told him.

"So what else is new?"

"Are you involved with Julian DiGeorgio?" Renee asked.

"Once upon a time," Cooper told her.

"Meaning what?"

"Meaning it was a long fucking time ago. DiGeorgio was a source back in the day. Nothing more."

"Well King is making a case that it was more than that and is trying to tie you into his narcotics operations."

"Renee, you know that's a bunch of bullshit."

"I know it, Cooper, but King is in MTAC pleading his case to the Director."

"Thanks for telling me. I've got something to trade."

"I'm all ears."

"Julian DiGeorgio is delivering drugs to Vinnie Calabresi up in San Clemente, using an outfit called Hi-Speed Delivery Services run by a mob guy named Leon DeGrassi. Calabresi has a rogue enforcer named Eddie Falcone that is trying to set DiGeorgio up for a fall," Cooper explained.

"No honor among thieves, eh?" Phillips asked.

"Not that you would notice, no," Cooper replied.

"You got caught up in a big fucking mess, didn't you?"

"I did."

"How are you going to get out of it?" Phillips asked.

"I'm still working on that," Cooper told her.

"I'm going to take what you just gave me up to King in MTAC and make sure the Director hears it too, maybe that will cool some of the heat off of you. At least on the legal side of things."

"Thank you, Renee. You're one of the good ones," Cooper told her before she hung up. He took another sip of his drink, leaning back on the couch. He had to figure out a plan.

~ ~ ~

Renee Phillips trotted up the stairs and put her eye to the retinal scanner that would unlock the door and allow her access to the room behind the door. The Director noticed her and acknowledged her, cutting King off in mid-sentence. "Agent Phillips, what have you got?" he asked.

"News. Julian DiGeorgio is shipping the drugs north to Vincent Calabresi using a local delivery service owned by another mob guy named Leon DeGrassi. It appears that one of Calabresi's people, an enforcer named Falcone, wants DiGeorgio's seat at the table," Phillips announced.

"You know this how?" the Director asked.

"I just got off the phone with Mitch Cooper. He's trying to save the life of a kid that was making the delivery."

"That sounds much more like the Mitch Cooper I know," the Director nodded. "King, back off and let Cooper do what he has to do. However, I want you ready to swoop in and pick up the pieces left after Cooper shakes them loose," the Director ordered.

"Aye, Sir," King growled, making it sound like Cur.

~ ~ ~

Eddie Falcone was waiting as Mike Gordon and Giselle Haskell pulled up beside him. He was leaning against his car, smoking a cigarette as Gordon exited his car. "How did you miss him?" Eddie asked.

"The private eye that Paloma hired was smarter than we realized. He got to Enrico and got him to dump Giselle," Gordon shrugged.

"What was his name again?" Eddie asked.

"Mitch Cooper, out of San Diego. He's got Enrico with him."

"Mike, you know I don't like failure, right?" Eddie asked softly.

"I know that, Eddie. Sometimes it just can't be helped. I'm hoping you'll give me a chance to make it right," Mike Gordon whispered.

"Normally, Mike, I wouldn't. This time, well you have one second chance. You bring me Rico's head, and Cooper's, and I will let you live. You fail me again, and I promise that you'll die screaming. You know what a turkey doctor is Mike?"

"Yeah, I've heard of them," Mike swallowed hard. Sure, he had heard of the turkey doctors. Guys who went to work on a guy that had screwed up and kept them alive long beyond what most humans could endure as they totally broke them. Mike had no desire to meet one.

"You don't bring me those two heads; I'm personally going to introduce you to one. The girl as well," Eddie told him.

"Sure thing, Eddie," Mike Gordon's face was blanched of all color. He decided that he wasn't going to tell Giselle

97

about the threat. It was bad enough that he had been forced to listen to it. Mike walked back to his car as if in a daze, climbed in, started the motor and drove away.

Eddie tossed his cigarette down and crushed it under his shoe. He got back in his car and headed back to San Clemente. He had stirred the pot. Now he would wait and see what came of it!

~ ~ ~

"Eddie, where the hell are you?" Vinnie Calabresi was yelling into the phone. Eddie Falcone moved it away from his ear and put it on speaker. At least that way he wouldn't lose an eardrum. Vinnie could get really loud when he wanted to.

"I'm still waiting on DiGeorgio's boys to meet me with the package. They still haven't shown up yet," Falcone said, grinning at the lie. No need to tell the boss that the package was in his trunk and the deliverymen were roasting in a burning car. Or had been the last he had seen of them.

"That fucking asshole, thinking he could pull this shit on me! I'm not gonna stand still for it, Eddie!"

"What do you want me to do, Mr. Calabresi?"

"I want you to hit that sonofabitch where he lives, that's what I want. I'm sending some boys down to give you a hand," Calabresi said.

"How about I try it my way first Boss? If it looks liked I need help, I'll call. Haven't I been sayin' all along that DiGeorgio ain't been showing you the proper respect," Falcone replied.

"You got twenty-four hours Eddie. Twenty-four. Bring me my money and my goods, or don't come back at all!"

"See you tomorrow, Boss," Falcone hung up. He lay

down on the motel room mattress and closed his eyes. Sleep came quickly.

~ ~ ~

"Mr. Calabresi? It's Marko," Gratziono said as he got his boss on the phone.

"Hey, Marko. I almost forgot I put you on Eddie's tail. He claims that Deej's boys never showed," Calabresi said. He heard a sharp intake of breath from Marko. "What is it, Marko? Is Eddie lying to me?"

"I don't like having to be the bearer of bad news, Mr. Calabresi."

"Just tell, me, Marko."

"Fast Eddie took out Mr. DiGeorgio's delivery crew and took the merchandise and the money. Then he laid up on a hill and was shooting into some house down in San Diego. He met that bent cop Gordon, and then went to the motel where he appears to have shut down for the night," Marko explained.

"Ah Jesus, Marko. I'm gonna give you over to Leo and I want you to give him the address of that motel. Make sure Fast Eddie don't leave," Calabresi said before handing the phone over to his houseman to get the address. He had a feeling that he knew exactly whose house Fast Eddie was shooting at earlier in the evening.

~ ~ ~

Julian DiGeorgio was furious! Somebody was taking potshots into his house! Not mention the crew he sent north was killed on the way. Something was starting to stink, and he didn't like the smell.

"Vito, your boys find anything up on the hill out back," he asked as Vito Molnari entered through the back door.

"Nothing but tire tracks, Boss. Whoever did this had it all planned out," Molnari shrugged.

"You get things squared away with the cops?"

"Yeah, put it off as some kids shooting off fireworks on the hill. They said they'd have a couple of extra patrols swing through."

"My tax dollars at work, eh Vito?"

"Well, they claim to protect and serve." Both of them laughed at that. The cops couldn't find their asses with both hands and a fucking flashlight. DiGeorgio's men were already spreading the word on the streets. Somebody knew something, and they would talk. One way or another.

The phone rang again. "Hey Boss, its Mr. Calabresi," Vito said, handing him the phone. "Hey, Vinnie. What can I do for you?" DiGeorgio asked.

"I heard you had some problems down your way tonight, and I'm pretty sure I know who is behind it," Calabresi told him.

"I'm listening," DiGeorgio said.

Chapter Thirteen

Cooper was up with the morning sun. He did a quick martial arts kata in the back yard followed by stretching and jumping jacks and push-ups until his body was covered in a light sheen of sweat, then he went back inside and took a shower, dressed, and went down to the kitchen to start coffee and breakfast.

Cooper was on his second cup of coffee and was finishing frying scrambled eggs in the bacon grease when Rico appeared in the kitchen. He was wearing clean clothes that Cooper had left out for him. He looked like a teenager in them. It made Cooper feel old.

"Breakfast?" Rico asked, looking surprised.

"The most important meal of the day, at least that's what the experts say," Cooper shrugged.

"It smells good."

"I'll make you plate. You may change your mind once you taste it," Cooper told him, piling eggs and several slices of bacon on a plate and setting it down in front of the kid.

"Thank you, Mister Cooper," Rico Verdes said.

"Rico, call me Mitch. Mister Cooper was my father. Silverware is in the drawer, you can get your own coffee," Cooper told him. He liked the kid. He was polite, and sharp, and he was finally thinking with more than his dick.

"Where did you learn to cook like this? I'm lucky to fry a hamburger," Rico said a few minutes later.

"I learned from my mom and dad. They said a man

should know how to make two meals well. First, he should know how to make at least one good supper dish, and then he should know how to make breakfast in case supper went really well. I took it to heart."

"Have you ever been married?"

"You're not my type, Rico."

"I wasn't suggesting it. I am merely curious."

"I was married once. A long time ago. I was still in the service. She didn't realize what that meant. She disappeared while I was overseas. The divorce papers were waiting when I came back. I didn't contest it. I figured it was for the best," Cooper sighed.

"It wasn't easy for you, was it?"

"Things like that never are. But it was for the best for her, and overall, it was the best for me as well."

"Do you ever question your decision?"

"Every day. In the end, the answer is always the same. Some people are made for marriage and happy ever after. I'm not one of them," Cooper shrugged.

"Do you think I did the right thing with Giselle? Ending it like that?" Rico asked.

"You did. She was only looking out for herself. That was why she stole the package to begin with."

"I guess."

"No guess, Rico. Truth."

"So, what do we do now? About Mr. DiGeorgio?"

"I'm still working on that," Cooper said.

"Am I going to die, Mitch?"

"Not if I can help it, Rico."

~ ~ ~

Marko yawned as he stretched. Fast Eddie's car was still

parked at the motel. He hadn't meant to go to sleep, but shit happened. If the car was there, the odds were that Eddie Falcone was too. His phone began to ring and Marko answered it. "Marko, is Fast Eddie still inside?"

"I ain't seen him leave, Leo," Marko replied. As far as he knew it was the truth. He sure as hell wasn't going to mention that he had gone to sleep.

"Okay. You keep watch. Me and the boys are going in," Leo said, breaking the connection. Marko lifted the binoculars that he had bought that had the built-in camera. He focused them on the room and started recording. He figured that this was something that Mr. Calabresi would want to watch. He spotted Leo and his crew as they went up the stairs to the room that Fast Eddie had rented. One of them blasted the lock with a shotgun and they went in. Marko frowned when no more shots followed. His phone rang again. It was Leo. Marko answered it.

"He ain't here, Marko. Why is that?" Leo asked.

"How the fuck would I know? I saw him go in, I didn't see him come out."

"Good. You can explain that to Mr. Calabresi," Leo said.

"I got no problem with that. We all knew that Eddie was a slick bastard," Marko growled.

"You better fucking hope so, Marko," Leo told him.

~ ~ ~

Fast Eddie Falcone frowned as he worked on a stack of pancakes at the IHOP. He had gotten a bad feeling during the night and went out the back window of his hotel room. Two blocks away he had called a taxi to pick him up and bring him to the restaurant. He had gotten a nervous tickle, a gut feeling that he couldn't afford to ignore.

He was certain he had done the right thing about getting the hell out of dodge. He ate a bite of pancake with blueberry syrup. It satisfied his sweet-tooth. There had been no calls from Vinnie. That pretty much confirmed the feeling that he had. Calabresi and DiGeorgio had figured out what he had planned and had teamed up. They were on to him. But that was okay, because Eddie intended to take them both out and take over both of their territories.

Eddie finished his meal and wiped his mouth with a napkin. He took a last drink of his coffee and asked for his check. He had things that he needed to pick up before he started killing off his competition. He would also have to avoid their crews that he knew were looking for him. What the hell, he always had enjoyed a challenge.

~ ~ ~

"Lara, when did Rico bring the truck back?" Leon DeGrassi asked as he walked through the front door.

"It was parked there when I got here and the keys had been dropped in through the mail-slot," Lara replied.

"You let anybody know yet?"

"I was waiting to see what you wanted to do."

"Okay. Go ahead and call the cops and let them know the van was brought back. I'll take care of the rest," DeGrassi said, walking back towards his office.

Lara smiled as she picked up the phone and dialed the San Diego Police Department. She asked for Detective Santos. He had been the one that had come to take the report when Leon had called in that the delivery van had been stolen. Santos seemed like an okay guy, much more so than his partner.

"Detective Santos," he answered.

"Detective Santos, this is Lara from Hi-Speed Delivery Service. Mr. DeGrassi wanted me to let you know that the missing van was returned to us during the night."

"That's great news. I'll make sure that the BOLO on it is cancelled. Any damages to the van?"

"Some scrapes on the rear bumper, not even enough to contact the insurance company about," Lara replied. She had checked the van over when she saw that it was back.

"Well thank you for letting us know. If you need anything else, I'm just a telephone call away," Santos told her.

"That's good to know," Lara told him before hanging up. She had kind of liked Santos. He was cute.

~ ~ ~

Leon DeGrassi settled into the leather chair behind his desk. He needed to let Julian know that the van had showed up, but so far not the kid. He wondered if Calabresi had gotten his package. If so, he might be able to talk Julian out of killing Rico. He was a good kid. That fucking Giselle was bad news. Leon had known that as soon as he had seen how hard the kid had fallen for her in such a short time. He scooped up his phone and dialed DiGeorgio's number.

Leon leaned back in his chair as the phone started to ring. DiGeorgio would be up by now. "Hello," said a voice on the other end.

"This is Leon DeGrassi, I have some news that I think Mister DiGeorgio is going to want to hear," he said.

"I'll get him. Hang on," the voice replied.

"What have you got, Leon?" Julian DiGeorgio's voice filled his ear.

"The van was back when I got here this morning, Sir,"

Leon said.

"That's interesting. Vinnie said the kid made his delivery and apologized for it being late," DiGeorgio mused.

"Mister DiGeorgio, Rico's a good kid. He's made good on everything. Do you think you might maybe show him a little mercy?" DeGrassi asked, swallowing hard.

"I'll consider it, Leon. But I make no promises. Thank you for letting me know," DiGeorgio said before hanging up. Leon DeGrassi said a little prayer for Rico, praying that Julian DiGeorgio would have mercy on the kid.

~ ~ ~

"Your brother brought Leon's truck back, and he made arrangements so that the package for Vinnie got delivered, even though it was late," DiGeorgio told Paloma as she walked into his home office.

"That is a good thing, isn't it?" Paloma asked, her eyes shining, tears gathering in them.

"It is. But only because it revealed that Fast Eddie Falcone is a rat."

"Will you spare Enrico for that?"

"I will have to think about that, Paloma. But things are looking far better for your brother than they were a day ago," DiGeorgio told her.

"Thank you, Julian," Paloma said.

"Don't thank me yet," he told her.

~ ~ ~

"Where do you think this asshole, Cooper has Rico?" Giselle asked.

"I wish I knew," Mike Gordon told her.

"We need to find them," Giselle growled.

"Believe me, I know that," Gordon said, thinking about

what Fast Eddie had said about the turkey doctor. He suppressed a shiver at the thought of it.

"This Cooper is supposed to be a private dick. You think he might be listed in the yellow pages?" Giselle asked. Gordon looked at her. He hadn't even thought about that. Sure, Cooper was a private eye. That meant he had to advertise, which meant he had an office and had to be listed somewhere so clients could find him.

"Giselle, you are a goddamn genius!" Gordon told her as he dug the San Diego telephone book out of the nightstand. He flipped through the yellow pages, looking for private detectives and investigators. He found Cooper's name on the third page. "Hot damn, here it is," he breathed.

"Here what is?" Giselle asked, glaring at him.

"The address for Cooper's office. He's in a strip mall just outside the Naval Air Station," Gordon told her.

"Which means what?" she asked.

"Which means we have a place to start looking," he told her.

~ ~ ~

"What the hell was that all about?" Detective Jake Arnold asked as he looked at his partner, Luke Santos.

"The missing delivery van turned up. Seems like it was returned to the delivery service this morning," Santos shrugged.

"That girl called you. The one out front," Arnold said knowingly.

"Lara. She seemed like a good girl."

"I bet. Did you know who owns that Delivery Service?"

"Some guy named DeGrassi."

"Do you know who DeGrassi is?"

"Besides owning the delivery service?"

"He's fucking connected, Kid. He's a fucking mobster," Arnold explained.

"To who?" Santos asked.

"Julian fucking DiGeorgio. The head man here in San Diego."

"Then I guess asking Lara out is off the table."

"It is if you're smart, Kid."

"Well fuck," Luke Santos sighed, leaning back in his chair.

"There are a lot of other women out there, Luke."

"I guess," Santos sighed.

~ ~ ~

Fast Eddie had managed to round up a car and several weapons. He had assembled enough to start a small war. He figured he would need every one of them if he was going to survive the next twenty-four hours. He was pretty sure that Vinnie was on his way down to San Diego at this point. The one place that he was likely to go was to Julian DiGeorgio's place.

It might give him a chance to kill two birds with one stone, so to speak. He liked the idea. It had a certain symmetry. He figured that by this time, Gordon had some sort of lead on Cooper.

Chapter Fourteen

Rico helped Cooper wash the dishes and put them up before he finally asked the question that had been on his mind since he had awakened. "What are we going to do to try and settle things with Julian DiGeorgio?"

"First, I'm going to call your sister and see if she can tell me how receptive DiGeorgio might be to making a deal," Cooper told him.

"You think Paloma will tell you the truth?"

"She hired me, remember? Plus she wants you home safe. If we can accomplish that, it will be along with a firm understanding that you both go through family counseling on boundaries."

"Good luck with that! Paloma doesn't recognize personal boundaries. She never has, not since we were small children."

"Are you saying that she is a little over-protective?"

"That would be like saying that the Titanic hit an ice cube," Rico sighed.

"Yeah, I had that impression as well. The thing is, kid, your big sister loves you and wants to protect you. She just doesn't realize that some of the ways she tries to protect you are why you end up in trouble," Cooper told him.

"Maybe," Rico finally admitted. Cooper grinned at him and pulled out one of his burner phones. He dialed Paloma's cell number from memory.

"Hello?" Paloma answered on the third ring.

"Paloma, this is Mitch Cooper. I need to ask you some questions about your brother," he told her.

"Have you found him?" she asked, her voice sounding urgent.

"Maybe. Will you answer my questions?"

"I will do the best I can."

"Good. First question, did anyone let Mr. DiGeorgio know that Rico's truck had been returned and that Mr. Calabresi did receive his original package?"

"Yes."

"How did Mr. DiGeorgio react to that news?"

"He appeared pleased by it."

"Is he regarding Rico in a more favorable light?"

"Yes, however he still maintains that Rico must be taught a lesson for what he did," Paloma sighed.

"That doesn't bode too well for your brother. Is there anything that might put Rico in a better light where DiGeorgio is concerned?"

"Somebody fired shots into the house last night. He has been on the phone all morning and Mr. Calabresi is coming down to San Diego this morning," Paloma said quietly, as if she were afraid of being overheard.

"Okay, I can work with that," Cooper told her before hanging up. Rico looked at him expectantly.

"Well?" he asked.

"Somebody is trying to stir things up between DiGeorgio and Calabresi. If we can figure out whom, and then give them to DiGeorgio in your place, it might buy you freedom from any retaliation," Cooper explained.

"Do you think it might be that guy Mike that Giselle told us about?" Rico wondered aloud.

"I think it might be whoever Mike was working for that had you set up."

"Who is that?"

"That is what we have to find out. Let's head to my office. I might be able to dig up more on Mike and figure out who he is working for."

"Okay," Rico agreed. They headed for the garage to collect the Eclipse.

~ ~ ~

Luke Santos frowned at the monitor on his desk. The whole thing about the van was just bothering him. The fact that it was mob-owned being beside the point. He had liked Lara. He wanted to see her again. He grabbed his jacket and shrugged it on. He noticed his partner looking at him from his own desk. "What?" Luke asked.

"You're gonna go see that girl, despite what I told you, aren't you?" Jake Arnold asked.

"I'm just following up on the theft report since the van was returned."

"Sure you are. And I'm gonna win an Oscar for best actor this year. What the hell, Kid. I guess I'll go along to keep you out of trouble," Jake Arnold sighed, heaving his bulk up out of his chair.

"Sure you will," Luke rolled his eyes, leading the way out of the squad room. The bosses had paired the two of them hoping that Santos would give them information that would lead to firing Jake Arnold. Instead, the two had liked each other and had become a very effective team, clearing a number of cases. Arnold had taken an interest in the kid and was teaching him all he knew, even though his retirement date was looming.

They walked out into the bright sunshine, a cool breeze blowing the air around. San Diego had a normal mean temperature around 75 degrees and little humidity. There was a reason that the city was called a west coast paradise.

Arnold took the passenger seat and let Luke drive. He had never let his previous partner drive, simply because she was a woman and more than likely would have gotten them killed. He shook his head, still not believing that Phillips had turned traitor and become an SDPD liaison to NCIS. All because of Mitch Cooper.

~ ~ ~

Fast Eddie Falcone was sitting in a parked car two blocks away from the home of Julian DiGeorgio. He was far enough away not to be noticed, but close enough to see what was happening at the Mob boss's house. His weapons were on the front seat beside him, but covered with a blanket in case anyone should walk past and happen to look inside his car.

DiGeorgio had no idea that Eddie had planted bugs all over the place on his last visit. He could hear everything going on inside. It sounded like DiGeorgio was calling a full war council, but not against Calabresi as he had hoped. No, Fast Eddie himself was the subject of the council.

He frowned. He didn't like that, not one damn bit. Apparently DiGeorgio and Calabresi had talked during the night or the early hours of the morning. That changed things, but not by much. He still planned to kill them both and take over their territories. He wanted to prove that a hotshot from the east that had been exiled to the west could rise to be a real boss!

~ ~ ~

Mike Gordon frowned as he sipped his coffee. He and Giselle were parked two lots down from the strip mall where Cooper maintained his office. All he could hope for was that Cooper would show up with Rico. He thought of Fast Eddie's threat of the Turkey Doctor and shuddered.

"Why are we sitting here wasting time?" Giselle asked, her face wrinkled up in a frown. Gordon didn't need to look at her to know that she was still pissed at Rico Verdes. And at Cooper. She wanted to kill them both, and Gordon was willing to let her pull the trigger. And as soon as she did, he planned on pulling the trigger on her. Giselle was too bat-shit crazy to let her live.

"Because Cooper has his office two lots down, and he eventually has to show up there, probably with Rico, unless he stashes him in a safe house somewhere. But if we get Cooper, we can make him take us to Rico," Gordon said.

"I want to take a knife to Cooper and cut his junk off and shove it down his throat," Giselle said, sounding cold and calm. Gordon suppressed a shiver of fear. Talk about a woman scorned! If she wanted to do that to Cooper, he hated to think what she might want to do to Rico!

"We need to make him talk first," Gordon reminded her.

~ ~ ~

Luke Santos pulled up to the curb across the street from the delivery service. "It looks pretty quiet for the moment. You going in to talk to your girlfriend?" Jake Arnold asked.

"I'm going in to talk to Lara, yes. However, Jake, she is not my girlfriend. We've only talked a couple of times," Luke said as he opened the door. He stepped out into the street.

"Keep telling yourself that," Jake called after him. Luke ignored him as he walked across the street to the front door of the delivery service. He pushed open the glass door and stepped inside.

He didn't see Lara anywhere yet as he removed his sunglasses and walked up to the counter. He figured that she could well be busy in the back. He rang the bell, announcing that there was somebody at the counter waiting on service. It was less than a minute before Lara appeared.

"Detective Santos, this is certainly unexpected," Lara flashed him a smile. He felt his legs go a little weak.

"Hi Lara, the Captain said that I should come by and do a follow up visit, even though the truck had turned up. You know how bosses are, wanting to dot all the eyes and cross all the tee's."

"You have that right," Lara rolled her eyes.

"I bet your boss is the same way," Luke grinned at her.

"You've got that right," Lara confided.

"So, when did you find out that the truck had been returned?" Luke asked her.

"I saw it when I showed up for work. I unlocked the place and found the keys inside the mail drop," Lara explained.

"Did you check out the truck?"

"I did. I wasn't so sure that I wouldn't find Rico dead in the back."

"But he wasn't?"

"No, the back of the truck was empty. All the packages had been delivered except for a box containing a stuffed rabbit for a little girl on Dana Point. All of the places on his route called to let us know," Lara explained.

"So what did your boss think when he found out the truck had turned up and all but one package had been delivered?" Luke asked

"He didn't know what to think, but I do know that he called Mr. DiGeorgio and told him about it."

"Have you told anyone else about this?" Luke asked.

"Not a soul but you," Lara told him, giving him a radiant smile.

"Here's my card. Please call me if you hear from Rico," Luke said.

"I promise," Lara flashed him another smile.

"Thank you," Luke told her. He turned and walked out of the office. The heat from the sun beat down on him as he slipped on his sunglasses and headed for the car. He opened the door and climbed inside.

"How did it go?" Jake asked.

"I got what we needed. DeGrassi called DiGeorgio. That means that both of them knew about the drug shipment. That ought to be enough to get us a warrant," Santos said as he put the car in gear and pulled away from the curb.

"That is some good work, Luke. The Captain is going to be happy about that news," Arnold nodded.

"That is what I figured too. What do you think that he will decide to do about it?"

"Your guess is as good as mine on that."

"That's what I figured," Luke sighed. Luke Santos didn't say so out loud, but he had a fair idea. DiGeorgio would want to teach the kid a lesson, even if he did make good on his promise and bring the truck back. He had a bad feeling as far as the kid's welfare was concerned.

~ ~ ~

Cooper had taken time to run by home and switch the Eclipse for the white ½ ton GMC Sierra before heading to the office. That was how he and Rico managed to get to the office without Giselle and Gordon spotting them. The two of them were looking for the red Eclipse.

"So what's the plan?" Rico asked as he took one of the chairs that Cooper reserved for clients.

"I'm going to do some computer searches and see what might be the best way to approach Julian DiGeorgio. I want to get you out of trouble with him, and hopefully get him to let Paloma go as well," Cooper explained.

"You really think you can do that?"

"I hope I can. If I can't get you both free of him, then there is always a chance that he will come after you both again," Cooper explained.

Chapter Fifteen

It was closing in on 9 o'clock in the morning as Cooper pulled the white GMC Sierra into the strip mall parking lot. The sun was shining and had already burned off the marine layer of fog from the bay. Fighter plans roared overhead as the Naval Air pilots practiced their maneuvers out of Coronado. Cooper had swung through a local coffee shop and got cups for both Rico and himself.

Cooper parked the truck and shut off the engine, climbing outside. Rico did the same and they walked to the front door of the office together. Cooper unlocked it and they went inside where Cooper disabled the alarm. Cooper turned his open sign around on the door and headed for his desk. Rico had already taken a seat in one of the two client chairs across the desk from Cooper's seat. Cooper booted up his computer. He looked at Rico. "You know how to work a coffee maker?"

"I think I can figure it out."

"Then please put a pot on. I've about finished what we picked up on the way here."

"I can do that," Rico called from the small room in the back that held a bank of file cabinets, a long table with a coffee maker and a small sink. There was also a small restroom before you got to the back room.

Cooper was busy logging into the TLOxp database used by licensed investigators across the country. He was going to see how many Mike's might live in San Clemente with connections in law enforcement and or ties to the mob. He had just hit the enter button when Rico came back in and took a seat across from him.

"So, have you figured out how to keep Mister DiGeorgio from killing me yet?" Rico asked.

"Not yet. Right now, I am looking for some additional leverage that we can use to get him off your back. It is not an easy task to begin with, but everybody has something that they want. We just have to figure out what DiGeorgio wants more than he wants you. Something we can trade for you," Cooper leaned back in his chair and waited while the computer did its thing.

~ ~ ~

"They just went into Cooper's office," Gordon told Giselle. She sat up straighter and leaned forward her eyes slitted like those of a hunting cat.

"Why are we still sitting here then?" Giselle hissed like an angry snake.

"We're going to give them a few minutes to get settled before we go in. We want them off-balance," Gordon explained to her. He could tell she didn't like it, but Giselle did give a barely perceptible nod. He took a deep breath and let it out slow. Time seemed to drag on forever as he let ten minutes' tick off the clock. Giselle was ready to explode with nervous tension and she nearly jumped out of her skin when he spoke again. "Now," he said.

She was out of the car almost before he had the door open. Giselle tapped her foot impatiently on the pavement as Gordon got out of the car. He could see that she had her hand on her gun in the purse that dangled from her shoulder. His own gun was tucked in his waistband under the over-sized aloha shirt he was wearing. He walked around the car and together they started towards the strip mall where Cooper's office was located.

~ ~ ~

"Anything?" Renee Phillips asked as she slipped into the back of the white Econoline Ford van that NCIS used for surveillance. There were magnetic stickers on the sides that currently identified it as belonging to San Diego Power and Light. Gabriel King was currently up a utility pole pretending to work on the transformer. What he was actually doing was wiring in a tap on the telephone line leading into DiGeorgio's house and scoping out the neighborhood at the same time.

"Nothing noticeable yet," King replied, sounding bored.

"I'm still finding it hard to believe that you actually got a warrant for this," Phillips shook her head.

"It helps when you know the right judge," King replied.

"I guess. What exactly do you think is going to happen?"

"I have no idea, but you can bet that this Falcone character is going to strike, either before or after Cooper contacts DiGeorgio."

"For somebody that claims to hate Cooper, you sure put a lot of faith in him," Phillips observed.

"I know Cooper. I know how he thinks. I also know that he will do what he says he'll do. If he can find a way to save the kid, he'll find a way to save the kid."

"Yes, Cooper is a man of his word. That's not something you see a lot of these days."

"You make it sound like it is a good thing."

"Somebody that keeps their word, yes, that is a good thing. Too many people these days don't understand honor.

Those Marines over at Camp Pendleton, they do," Phillips shrugged, knowing that King couldn't see her actions.

"Yes, they do. Thanks for reminding me of that, Phillips," King sighed.

"My pleasure," she said with a smile. Sometimes King needed the reminder that he wasn't the only Marine in the world. She thought about dialing Cooper and then decided not to. He had enough on his plate with trying to save that kid.

~ ~ ~

Paloma Verdes could sense the tension in the house. Julian had suggested that she might want to leave and take a day at the spa. She had refused. She knew that Cooper would be calling to try and make a deal for her brother. She needed to be there to help persuade Julian to take the deal. She would not leave.

Julian had tried to tell her that it was too dangerous for her to remain, that Don Calabresi was coming to talk, and that one of his enforcers had gone crazy and wanted to kill Calabresi and him. Paloma told him that didn't matter. That her place was with her man. Julian had accepted that as a matter of course, not even suspecting her true desire to remain at the house.

Oh, he had tried to lie and tell her that since the drugs had been delivered and the truck returned that he no longer had any interest in poor Enrico. But in her heart, Paloma knew better. She knew that unless Cooper could come up with some kind of miracle, that her brother was living on borrowed time. If it came down to it, she would murder Julian herself to spare her brother's life.

She headed to the kitchen and poured herself a glass of

iced tea, and then carried it back to Julian's office. She wanted to keep an eye on this man that held not only her fate, but her brothers as well, in his hands. She wanted to make sure that Rico could be saved even if she had to sacrifice herself to make it happen.

~ ~ ~

Fast Eddie Falcone looked at his watch. He would have thought that Vinnie would be there by now. That was okay. He could afford to be patient. He would strike once he had the two bosses together in one spot. Two birds with one stone, and then he would pin it all on Gordon and the girl.

It was a good plan. He had picked up some special ordnance from a guy at Coronado. Stuff that DiGeorgio and Calabresi certainly wouldn't be expecting. Falcone planned to hit them like lightning, shock and awe in modern terms, but he preferred the old term. *Blitzkrieg,* or lightning war in German. The Nazis had perfected it in the Second World War. But Eddie planned to adapt it to his current mission. He would cut down two of the bosses, and then he would take their place, like a phoenix arising from the ashes!

~ ~ ~

The computer beeped and Cooper looked up. There was a cop, currently on suspension from the San Clemente OCB unit named Mike Gordon. That explained a lot. That was how Mike knew about the dope shipment. He was on Calabresi's payroll. Apparently, Fast Eddie Falcone had made him a better offer, and Gordon had set Rico up to take the fall for him.

"What is it?" Rico asked.

"We have our leverage, my young friend," Cooper smiled. Just then, the front door of his office opened and

Mike Gordon and Giselle Haskell stepped into the waiting area with guns drawn.

"Well, look who we found! See, Giselle, I told you we'd find them here," Detective Mike Gordon said with a smirk on his face.

"So, what? You want a damn ticker tape parade for being right?" Giselle replied.

"No, not really. Rico, Cooper, you boys have caused us a world of trouble," Gordon told them.

"It seems to me that it is the other way around," Cooper replied nonchalantly, leaning back in his chair. His mind was racing, trying to figure out some kind of plan. Drawing his gun was problematical since it was holstered on his hip and if he dropped his hand out of sight it would likely earn him a bullet.

"I don't appreciate being used, Giselle," Rico said, standing, drawing their attention to him. It was all that Cooper needed. He scooped up his coffee cup and threw it at Giselle, then dropped his right hand to the butt of the Beretta holstered to draw it and aim and fire. The first shot caught Gordon in the shoulder and spun him around.

Rico jumped Giselle while she was blinded by the hot coffee and wrestled her pistol away from her. He had her covered as Cooper came around the desk and moved on the fallen detective from San Clemente. Cooper kicked Gordon's gun away from his hand as Gordon groaned and tried to sit up. "Rico, there are some plastic zip-tie style cuffs in the top drawer of my desk. I'll cover these two while you get out a couple of them," Cooper said. Gordon glared up at him with eyes full of hate.

Rico had stuffed Giselle's pistol into his waistband

behind his right kidney and fastened the zip-tie around her wrists, securing them behind her back. Cooper had Gordon roll over and Rico secured his hands as well, before dragging them over against the wall, where he secured their ankles as well. Cooper holstered his pistol.

"Guys, that was really rude, the way you came in here waving guns and everything," Cooper told them.

"I have to agree with him," Rico added, nodding.

"Fuck you Rico!" Giselle spat.

"Why don't you shut up? Cooper, you have a roll of duct tape around here, somewhere don't you?" Rico asked.

"I do. Over in the top drawer of the filing cabinet," Cooper directed him. "I agree with Rico, Giselle. I'm more interested in what Detective Gordon can tell me than in anything you might have to say.

Giselle started to say something, but Rico slapped the strip of duct tape over her mouth and smoothed it down. She tried to curse at him, but all that came through was a bunch of high-pitched noises. Rico turned and grinned at Cooper before heading back to the chair he had occupied earlier.

Cooper winked at him before centering his attention on Gordon once more. "So, Gordon, tell me about the deal you have with Fast Eddie Falcone."

"What deal?" Gordon's face had gone pale and sweat was breaking out on his forehead. Of course, that *could* have been because of the bullet hole in his shoulder.

"The one where you are knocking off a lot of Fast Eddie's competition to help him rise up in the Calabresi family. Word on the street has it that Eddie wants to take Julian DiGeorgio's spot at the table. That sound about right to you, Mikey?" Cooper asked

"You need to call the cops and turn us over to them. I know my rights, Cooper," Gordon said stubbornly.

"Rights? Did he seriously just try to invoke his rights?" Cooper looked at Rico.

"It sounded like it to me," Rico nodded.

"I really don't think he understands his position."

"I think I would agree with that."

"Do you think I should maybe clarify it for him?"

"I don't see any reason not to. I mean, not only is this guy a bad cop, but he's a traitor as well, selling dope to Marines."

"Agreed. Hey, Gordon, which is your strong leg? Right or left?" Cooper asked, drawing his pistol once more.

"What?" Gordon looked up at him as if he were insane.

"Right or left?" Cooper asked again.

"Why?"

"Well, if you must know, which takes all the fun out of it I may add, I am about to shoot you in the knee cap. So, which one would you prefer to lose, right or left?" Cooper asked again.

"Neither!" Gordon looked panicked now.

"Then start talking," Cooper told him.

Chapter Sixteen

Fast Eddie Falcone watched through a pair of binoculars as Vinnie Calabresi and his crew of hard men arrived. The guys with him were his palace guard, the royal retune. Every one of them would willingly give their lives to protect their boss. Eddie wasn't the least surprised. He had counted on it. If he could take all of them out, along with Calabresi and DiGeorgio and his palace guard, then it would be easier for him to step in and pick up the pieces.

Eddie wondered how Gordon was coming along with finding Rico. He knew that he had motivated the man. He was surprised that he hadn't got a phone call already. Eddie shook his head. Good help was getting hard to find...

~ ~ ~

"So, what do you think?" Luke Santos asked Jake Arnold.

"I think that we got some kind of fucking gang war brewing," Arnold replied

"DiGeorgio and Calabresi?" Luke asked.

"Maybe, maybe not. Could be some upstart wanting to stir the pot. Let's go see Julian DiGeorgio," Jake said.

"Are you sure that is a good idea?" Luke looked at his partner.

"Best one I have for now," Jake shrugged.

"Okay. Do you have his address? I mean, it might help to know where I'm going."

"Change seats, I'll drive. Most of us old guys know

where the mob guys live, and it's just easier to drive than to give you directions."

~ ~ ~

Three Hummer H3's pulled onto DiGeorgio's street and rolled in a convoy toward his house. They were all black, and it was a good bet that they were every bit as armored as what U.S. Forces used overseas. King frowned. He hated the idea of these pieces of shit using the same vehicles for transport that soldiers used fighting for their country. It made him mad, even though there was nothing he could do about it.

"It looks like Calabresi and his people have arrived," he told Phillips through his com unit.

"Sounds like the party is about to get started," she replied. Renee Phillips was watching the arrival on the video feed that King had rigged to the pole.

"Yeah, no sign of Cooper yet. However, there is a Chevy Lumia parked about two blocks down that is making me twitchy. You want to check it out?" King asked her.

"I can do that," Renee said, glad for a chance to get out of the van and move around a bit. The passengers were exiting from the three Hummers and heading for DiGeorgio's place. Julian had even stepped outside to greet them.

~ ~ ~

Jake Arnold pulled onto the street driving slow as he scanned the scene in front of him with a policeman's eye. He spotted the three Hummers parked out front. "Will you look at that? I think maybe the party started without us."

"What do you mean?" Luke asked.

"See those Humvee's up ahead? Those belong to Vinnie

Calabresi. It appears that we may have just rolled up on a powwow between him and DiGeorgio."

"So, what do you want to do now?"

"I think now we park and watch and wait to see what goes down."

"You want me to call it in?"

"Not yet," Arnold replied as he pulled to the curb and parked, shutting off the engine after taking the car out of gear.

~ ~ ~

Renee Phillips had crossed the street and was walking down the sidewalk on the opposite side of the road from DiGeorgio's place. She saw the Lumia that King had mention, but she had also noticed the unmarked white Dodge Charger that had pulled onto the street and parked. She keyed her mike. "Looks like local cops have shown up as well," she told King.

"Fucking wonderful! So far, it looks like everybody but Cooper has shown up to this shindig," King sighed. Phillips grinned, sensing his disappointment in his voice.

"Hey, I'm just the messenger. Though I am seeing some movement in the Lumia," Phillips told him.

"What kind of movement?" King asked.

"Looks like the guy is finally getting out of his car," she said, moving closer.

~ ~ ~

"That was a pretty interesting story, Gordon," Mitch Cooper said. He still held the Beretta loosely in his hand.

"It's the truth," Gordon sighed.

"I hope so. I'm about to call Julian DiGeorgio, and when I get him on the phone, you are going to tell him everything

127

that you just told me," Cooper told him.

"Sure, why not?" Gordon sighed in defeat.

"Well, if you don't, you lose first your left knee cap, and then your right. And if that doesn't do it, I'll do your elbows next. Either you'll tell the truth or you'll be crippled for life," Cooper shrugged.

Giselle was still squirming in her seat, but to no avail. Rico was keeping a close eye on her. He trusted her about as much as he trusted an angry rattlesnake in his bed. Cooper picked up the office phone and dialed Julian DiGeorgio's number.

~ ~ ~

Fast Eddie paid little attention to the woman coming down the sidewalk toward him. She was unimportant in the larger scheme of things. He opened the rear door of his car and reached inside, pulling out a fiber-glass tube about a yard long. He removed the end-caps from the tube and pulled on it, freeing the pop-up sights. Eddie aimed the tube at Julian's house and squeezed the trigger mechanism. Flame spurted from both ends of the tube and the LAWS rocket shot away from the car. The rearmost of the Humvee's lifted into the air on a ball of flame and thunderous noise.

Eddie discarded the tube and pulled out another one. He followed the same procedure with a fluid economy of motion and this time sent the warhead rocketing into the front of DiGeorgio's house. Flame and glass filled the air. He smiled as he imagined the confusion taking place inside his target. He pulled out an AK-47 and flipped the safety lever from safe to full auto and began hosing the house down with the fifty-round magazine.

Bullets shattered his front windshield, and Fast Eddie spun to meet the new threat. He squeezed the trigger, sending six rounds blasting at the woman with the pistol. He saw her dive for cover as he buttoned out the curving magazine. He pulled out a fresh one and hammered it home. He pulled back the bolt and blasted away at her, driving her deeper under cover. He heard car doors open behind him, and Fast Eddie spun around, his assault rifle blasting away.

The windshield of the unmarked police car imploded under the impact from the AK's rounds. The two cops, scrambled behind the vehicle as he raked it with fire. Fast Eddie dived into his car, fired the engine, threw it in gear and stomped on the gas! He burnt rubber getting into motion, the rear end of the car fish-tailing as it moved down the street. In seconds, the street was quiet, except for the crackle of flames from burning vehicles and the front of Julian DiGeorgio's house.

~ ~ ~

"What the fuck, Julian?" Vinnie Calabresi was yelling even as DiGeorgio dragged him deeper inside the house and away from the chaos that had exploded through the front window.

"Damned if I know, Vinnie. We definitely have us a problem," DiGeorgio rasped. "I think it may be Fast Eddie."

"Probably. He's been making a lot of noise, lately. Especially about how he wants to take over your territory," Vinnie admitted.

"And you are just telling me this now?" DiGeorgio asked.

"It didn't seem relevant before," Vinnie shrugged.

"I bet," DiGeorgio raged.

~ ~ ~

Renee Phillips climbed to her feet. She had taken cover behind a walled in planter when the shooter had targeted her. She had managed to get a good look at the shooter and she could identify him as Fast Eddie Falcone.

"Phillips, are you okay?" King's voice was loud in her ear.

"He missed me," she told him.

"What about the two cops?"

"Unfortunately, he missed them too," Phillips sighed.

"What the hell do you mean by that?" King asked.

"One of them is my ex-partner."

"Well shit."

"Exactly."

~ ~ ~

"What the fuck just happened?" Luke Santos asked his partner. Both were crouched behind what was left of their unmarked police car, guns drawn.

"How the hell should I know?" Jake Arnold growled back.

"You guys just blew my stakeout is what happened," Renee Phillips announced.

"Renee?" Jake Arnold sounded surprised.

"The one and only, Jake," Renee replied.

"Then I suppose that psycho from NCIS is nearby as well?" Arnold sighed, rolling his eyes.

"Yes, Jake, and he can hear every word you say, so you might want to dial it back on the name calling."

"Luke, call this in. Phillips, you got any idea who that asshole that shot up our car was?" Arnold asked her.

"His name is Eddie Falcone. He appears to be trying to start a war between Calabresi and DiGeorgio."

"You care if we put out an APB on him?"

"Go for it. Eddie is not our primary concern now."

"Good to know. And Renee?"

"Yeah?"

"Thanks," Arnold said, meaning it for once in his life.

~ ~ ~

Fast Eddie was powering away from Julian DiGeorgio's neighborhood as fast as he could manage. He didn't want to speed and alert the police. They were probably looking for his car already thanks to the two cops that had pulled up behind him. He shook his head. Bad fucking luck. It seemed to be hovering over him like a cloud right now. Well, he could change his luck. And he would take out DiGeorgio, and maybe Vinnie as well. One thing was for sure though. Fast Eddie was going to make a name for himself in Mob circles, one fucking way or another!

~ ~ ~

"Hey Cooper, you might want to check this out before you make that call," Rico said. He had flipped the television over to the local news.

"What have you got?" Cooper asked, walking over to see what Rico was watching.

"Less than an hour ago, a mysterious military-style attack was launched on the residence of investment banker Julian DiGeorgio while he was meeting with his associate Vincent Calabresi. One police car was targeted for unknown reasons, but the information office has refused to release the names of the officers involved," the anchorperson announced.

"Yeah, this might not be the best time to call. Especially since half of the San Diego P.D. is camped out on DiGeorgio's lawn." From the video, it appeared that DiGeorgio's house had taken significant damage from what appeared to have been a rocket attack.

"So, what do we do now?" Rico asked.

"How about you take my truck and make a run to get us all lunch? There is a Mickey D's about three blocks down the road. Go grab us lunch," Cooper told him, handing him a pair of twenties.

"I'll be back in a flash," Rico said, heading out the door, Cooper's keys clutched tightly in his fist. Cooper looked at his two unwilling guests.

"You two may as well get comfortable. You're going to be here a while," Cooper told them. Both glared at him over their taped mouths.

~ ~ ~

Rico drove to the nearest McDonalds and placed his order. He was surprised that Cooper had trusted him enough to do so. Cooper didn't seem to like letting other people take control, not even over little things. Then he figured it out. Cooper trusted him. That was cool. He would do his best not to betray that trust. He picked up the order when it was called and headed back to Cooper's office.

Chapter Seventeen

"**W**e need to do something about Fast Eddie, Julian," Vinnie Calabresi said as he sipped at the cup of coffee that DiGeorgio had made him.

"Yes, we do. But we gotta be smart about it. Fast Eddie was sent out here for a reason, and neither of us knows exactly who back east is sponsoring him," DiGeorgio said.

"That's a good point, Julian. What I am wondering though, is why he was sent west? Did somebody realize that they had a fucking time bomb on their hands and want to pawn him off on one of us?"

"That is a good question. I know a couple of guys back east that might be able to shed some light on things. I'll give them a call and see what the hell that they come up with."

"That sounds like a good idea."

"I thought so too."

"I thought you might. As of right now, though, I am putting out paper on Fast Eddie Falcone," Julian announced.

"I'll match whatever amount you put on him," Calabresi said. "And I want the word to go out nationwide!"

"Good idea. We'll get the word out that Fast Eddie is not to be trusted, and that the contract is an open one," DiGeorgio said.

~ ~ ~

"So, what are we going to do with these two?" Rico asked after returning with the food. Cooper pulled out a small fry and a double bacon cheese burger before he answered. Unwrapping the cheese burger, he dumped the fries out onto the wrapper to make them easier to get to.

"We have a couple of options, probably none of which they are going to like," Cooper replied.

"I can see that," Rico nodded knowingly.

"First, we could offer them to Calabresi and DiGeorgio in exchange for them leaving you alone."

"I kind of like that one."

"I thought you might. Or, we could turn them over to the cops where they would probably be locked up for a long time."

"I like the sound of that one as well," Rico nodded. "Not as much as option number one of course."

"Understandable. Option three is we could just take them out on a boat and feed them to the sharks and nobody would be the wiser," Cooper explained.

"Again, I can't find fault with that one either. However, I can see what you mean about them not liking any of the options," Rico nodded.

"So, should we put it to a vote?" Cooper asked, his eyes twinkling with humor while he kept his expression deadpan.

"Votes for number three?" Rico asked, raising his hand. Cooper raised his as well but the two prisoners became very loud as they tried to protest through the duct tape over their mouths.

"Looks like a tie on three," Cooper noted.

"In favor of option two?" Rico raised his hand again, as did Cooper. Again, the prisoners protested.

"Another tie. If it happens again I'll just flip a coin,"

Cooper sighed.

"That just leaves option number one," Rico raised his hand as did Cooper. This time the captives were quiet.

"We have a winner," Cooper observed.

"So, it appears. I guess now is as good a time as any to make the call," Cooper said, reaching for the telephone on his desk. He dialed the number for DiGeorgio's house. It rang twice before it was being answered. "I need to speak to Mr. DiGeorgio," Cooper said.

The mobster was on the line in thirty seconds. "Fast Eddie is this you?" DiGeorgio demanded.

"Afraid not, Mr. DiGeorgio. However, I have a couple of people who would be willing to tell you everything they know about Fast Eddie Falcone," Cooper told him.

"I'm listening," DiGeorgio said.

"I'm willing to give them to you in exchange for something."

"How much?" DiGeorgio sounded tired.

"No cash. I just want you to leave Enrico Verdes alone. He let a woman get into his head and screw him up. But he made the delivery and returned the truck. I'll let you have the woman and Falcone's pet cop in exchange for that," Cooper explained.

"How long do I have to think about it?" DiGeorgio asked.

"How long do you think it will take Eddie to make another run at you? I'm thinking the pet cop may know more about his plans than what he has admitted to me. It's your choice," Cooper said.

"Call me back in fifteen minutes," DiGeorgio said, hanging up. Rico looked at Cooper expectantly.

"Well?" he asked.

"He wanted a few minutes to consider his options," Cooper replied.

"What do you think he's going to do?"

"I don't know, but I can maybe make a guess or two."

"So, give me your best guess."

"I think he'll go for it. But with these wiseguys you never can tell. However, I think your sister has already been talking to him, trying to get him to leave you alone. This may just provide the incentive he needs to tip the scales in your favor," Cooper explained.

"Somehow, that just isn't real comforting. Not as much as I hoped it might be," Rico sighed.

"Maybe not. It is, however, cause for hope. Hope and faith can move mountains my friend."

"I hope you're right," Rico sighed.

~ ~ ~

Gabriel King had come down from his pole and stood leaning against the white Econoline van as Phillips returned. "Phillips, that was a first class fuck up if I ever saw one," he shook his head.

"Really? Tell me what you would have done differently," Phillips met his glare with one of her own.

"Not a damn thing," King admitted. "The problem was the arrival of you SDPD buddies. They flushed him early."

"Believe me I let them know that. Right now, they are explaining their actions to a very unsympathetic watch commander," Phillips grinned.

"Good Girl. I knew that there was *something* about you that I liked."

"Flattery will get you nowhere," Phillips said.

"Yeah, I get that," King sighed.

"I hope so," Phillips replied.

~ ~ ~

"Vinnie, I may have a handle on Fast Eddie," Julian DiGeorgio said.

"A handle? Talk to me," Vinnie Calabresi said.

"Some guy just called, said he had Fast Eddie's pet cop who could tell us Fast Eddie's plans."

"What does he want?"

"He wants me to let the delivery driver alone."

"I want you to let him alone. The kid came through, and I heard he took the truck back. If leaving him alone gives us Fast Eddie's plans, well it sounds like a good deal to me."

"You think so?"

"You don't?"

"I don't fucking know what to think," DiGeorgio sighed.

"The delivery guy is not our enemy, Deej. Fast Eddie is," Calabresi said.

"Okay then, I'll make the deal when he calls back."

"Do that."

~ ~ ~

Fast Eddie had put some distance between himself and DiGeorgio's place. He hadn't counted on the cops showing up when they had. Was it bad luck? Or was it something else? Had Gordon spilled his guts? It was possible. Fast Eddie didn't like that one little bit. But how could Gordon have gotten to DiGeorgio so fast? He frowned. He had a couple of other stops to make before he circled back around to DiGeorgio. But those stops certainly wouldn't make DiGeorgio happy.

He was headed for a specific residence on Brookhaven

Road in Bay Terraces. It was one of DiGeorgio's clearing houses for narcotics distribution. It was time to hit ol' Deej where it hurt, in the moneybags!

~ ~ ~

"Mister DiGeorgio, please," Cooper said when the telephone was answered.

"One moment," the man that answered told him. Cooper waited patiently.

"Is this the guy that wanted to make the deal?" Julian DiGeorgio's voice asked.

"Indeed, it is."

"You've got a deal. Where do I pick up the pet cop and the girl?"

"How about the pier in Oceanside?" Cooper asked.

"When?" DiGeorgio asked.

"One hour."

"How will I know you?"

"I'll know you and make the approach," Cooper told him and then hung up. He looked at Rico. "It's a good. Terms were agreed to."

"That is certainly a relief," Rico said.

"You're free to go then Rico. You're off the hook," Cooper told him.

"I'll see it through, Mitch. If you don't mind," Rico replied, his expression sober.

"You don't have to."

"I know that. But it is my own fault that I got mixed up in this mess. So, I want to see it through to the end," Rico told him.

"I think I can understand that. Check Gordon's pockets for keys and go out and see if you can figure out which vehicle these two came in.

"I can do that."

"Good, because otherwise we'd have to throw these two in the back of my truck and that is not something that I want to have to explain to the police should we have a traffic stop."

"That makes perfect sense to me," Rico said as he took possession of Gordon's keys and headed out the door. Cooper looked down at the two prisoners.

"You guys are amateurs at this. You should never mess with professionals," Cooper told them. Rico was back within five minutes.

"They had a nice four door sedan parked two lots down. It is now parked right outside the door," Rico said as he re-entered the office.

"Rico, take this gun and cover them, you can take the tape off of Gordon. You might want to leave Giselle's mouth taped shut. If they try to escape, drop them where they stand."

~ ~ ~

Fast Eddie made the walk from his car to the door in a couple of seconds. He rapped hard on the wooden door, looking bored, his eyes covered by dark sunglasses.

The door opened and Eddie pushed inside, shoving the doorman back as he pushed inside. "Deej sent me," Eddie said as he headed for the packaging and distribution room. The doorman looked flustered and didn't know what to do. So, he backed off as Fast Eddie headed for the vault where the cash was kept.

Eddie acted like he was in charge and five minutes later he was back in the car with a couple of hundred thousand in cash.

Five minutes after he left, the bomb he had left inside exploded and killed the employees and set most of the drugs in the place on fire. Eddie smiled in the rear-view mirror as he saw the black smoke rising up into the sky.

DiGeorgio was not going to be happy about that. He was going to burn the king of San Diego's house down around his fucking ears! He had another stop to make before he circled back around to DiGeorgio. This one in Chula Vista.

~ ~ ~

Jake Arnold and Santos were back at the precinct house when the call came in from Bay Terraces. Jake looked across his desk at Santos. "That's one of DiGeorgio's places," he said.

"Sounds like somebody has it in for this DiGeorgio guy in a serious way," Luke said.

"I think you might be right about that," Arnold nodded.

"Should we roll on it?"

"After the ass-chewing we just got? You've gotta be fucking kidding me! We are out of this mess kid. Let the golden boys handle it," Jake Arnold sighed.

"You can be a real ass when you want to be, Jake," Luke glared at him.

"You goddamn well better believe it, Kid. If you roll on it, you do so on your own. I'm too goddamn close to retirement to fuck around with this," Jake Arnold told him.

Chapter Eighteen

It didn't take long for Cooper and Rico to get Gordon and Giselle out and into Gordon's car. Under the threat of being shot, they were very cooperative. Cooper slipped behind the wheel and left Rico to keep an eye on the two prisoners.

"So how are we supposed to do this?" Rico asked.

"We meet them and then hand these two over and drive away," Cooper replied.

"That simple?"

"That simple," Cooper nodded.

"What happens if they decide to take us out at the hand off?" Rico asked.

"I have a plan for that."

"Would you care to let me in on it?"

"Not yet. And certainly, not in front of these two. I'll let you know in advance of the hand off."

"Well, that's reassuring."

"I thought it might be," Cooper grinned.

"Cooper," Rico said, his voice fading.

"Just look at this as a learning experience."

"A learning experience? Really?"

"Sure, you honestly don't think you can go back to work for DeGrassi after this?"

"I hadn't thought about it really," Rico admitted.

"You seem to have good instincts, and I can use a partner and apprentice."

"Is that a job offer?"

"It is. You don't have to answer right now, but at least take a few days and thinking about it."

"I can do that," Rico nodded. He leaned back in the seat, not quite sure what to think. Enrico Verdes, Private eye. He grinned. It had a nice ring to it. He wondered what Paloma might think about it. More than likely, she would think that it would be too dangerous and beneath him. However, it intrigued him. To him, it sounded like a new opportunity to explore. One that he was very interested in.

~ ~ ~

"Do you think this is a good idea, Boss?" Leo Capuleto asked.

"I do," DiGeorgio answered.

"What if this is a set up?"

"I don't think it is, Leo."

"You think this guy really has Fast Eddie's pet cop?" Leo asked. His job was to protect his boss no matter what. Even to the point of dying to protect him if it came to that.

"I believe him, Leo. He wants to save the kid. Throwing us a decoy doesn't do that. So yeah, I buy it," Julian DiGeorgio told him.

"Okay, but Benji Matorelli and Arty Carpezi are loyal. I trust both with my life."

"If you say so," Leo responded.

"I say so," DiGeorgio told him.

~ ~ ~

Luke Santos was by himself as he made a soft probe in Julian DiGeorgio's neighborhood. He had left Jake Arnold behind, and he wasn't at all proud of it. Arnold was old school, but he wasn't willing to take any risk that might cause him his pension. Arnold was counting the days until his retirement.

Luke wasn't. He actually wanted to make a difference in the world. More than likely, Arnold would throw him to the wolves. Except Luke didn't care. He wanted to take out the bad guys. How he did it, well that really didn't matter!

~ ~ ~

Jake Arnold leaned back in his chair. His ass felt sore from the chewing that had been done on it earlier. He had told Luke that he didn't care. That he just wanted to put in his time. But he also knew that it wasn't true. He liked Luke Santos. The man was his partner. He hated leaving him hanging out to dry. He hated the fact that he had found himself in another of Mitch Cooper's cases, even after the fact.

Cursing himself, he climbed out of his chair and headed for the motor pool. Luke was out there by himself. That was Jake's fault. He intended to rectify the situation. One way or another!

~ ~ ~

Mike Gordon looked at his feet. There really wasn't a whole lot more that he could do. Especially with his hands cuffed behind his back. The same was true of Giselle. They no longer had any options. Death was inevitable as taxes. Would he talk? More than likely he would, if only in a chance to save himself. But he found that he wanted to save Giselle as well.

He didn't know why, or how. But at some point, he and Giselle had connected on some sort of elemental level. Perhaps they had been united in their hate for Mitch Cooper, but he really didn't have an answer.

~ ~ ~

"Here," Cooper said as he pulled off to the side of the road. Rico exited from the passenger side even as Cooper exited the driver's side. They moved to the rear of the car and Cooper unlocked the trunk.

"Talk to me, Mitch. What the hell is this all about?" Rico asked him.

"Our friends in the back are part of a plan to disrupt and destroy the American way of life. You know this yes?" Cooper asked.

"I do."

"So, what do you intend to do about it?"

"I wish I knew."

"Do you trust me, Rico?" Cooper asked.

"You pretty much saved my life so yeah, I guess I do," Rico replied.

"I'm not really going to toss these two to the wolves. Not without at least giving them a chance to fight back and maybe survive." Cooper pointed into the open trunk. There were several weapons inside. "See anything you know how to use?"

"Actually, I do," Rico grinned scooping up a pistol-gripped Mossberg 500 Persuader 12-guage shotgun. He worked the pump one-handed to load a round into the chamber.

"Okay, now what about a handgun?"

"Revolvers are pretty simple, right?"

"Yes, they are."

"This one, then," Rico picked up a 4-inch barreled Smith & Wesson 686 in .357 Magnum. He stuffed it into his waistband. "What about them?" he asked.

"I've got a couple of .22 automatics that I'm going to slip into their pockets at the exchange. I figure after that, they are on their own," Cooper replied.

"That makes sense," Rico agreed. "Mitch, did you really mean it about hiring me and taking me on as a partner?"

"I did. Sometimes I get cases that take me to places where I stand out because I'm older. I need somebody who can go and blend in. You fit that bill. Plus, I like the way you handle yourself," Cooper explained.

"Okay. I just needed to know if you were serious. I'll take the job."

"Then you are officially on the payroll. Let's do this and get this thing wrapped up," Cooper said.

~ ~ ~

Luke Santos was where he could keep a weather eye on the DiGeorgio house, or what was left of it. He was amazed that DiGeorgio's men were actually boarding up windows and keeping their boss inside. He would have thought they would leave, go to a harder compound that was easier to defend.

Luke watched as another car pulled on the street and rolled slowly by. It looked like one of the unmarked cars, but he couldn't be sure. He shook his head. He figured he was probably the only cop on the force crazy enough to put himself in the middle of what could turn out to be a bloodbath. Luke sighed. He was here by choice, his choice. Because he believed that the shooter from earlier would come back. Luke wanted to be the cop that took him down, once and for all.

~ ~ ~

Jake Arnold rolled down the street. His eyes were

sweeping back and forth over the street. He hadn't spotted Luke yet. Maybe that was a good thing, because it meant that the kid had found a good spot to observe from. But he knew his partner was out there. He would find him. Jake Arnold was not about to let his partner get killed in a mob war!

Jake pulled the car over to the curb and cut the engine. He sat there waiting. He could hear the engine of the car ticking as it cooled in the evening air. Arnold opened the door and stepped out into the evening air. If he was going to find Luke, he would have to do it on foot.

~ ~ ~

Julian DiGeorgio walked out of the house accompanied by a full crew of ten men. They climbed into three cars and pulled out of the driveway moving in a convoy. DiGeorgio was in the middle car. They were headed for Oceanside Pier. The guy on the phone had wanted to make the turn over to him personally to guarantee the boy's safety. DiGeorgio could respect that. He also knew that it would make Paloma happy.

Why that was such a concern, he didn't know. It surprised him that it was. Paloma was an exceptional woman. He was surprised to discover that her feelings actually mattered to him. Was he becoming soft in his old age? Or could it be that he had finally found a woman worthy of falling in love with? It was something he would consider as he went to pick up Fast Eddie's pet cop!

Julian had suspected that Eddie had eyes on his territory for a while. It was something that the young Turk from New York hadn't been able to hide. A man could see the blind desire in his eyes. Fast Eddie wouldn't stay hidden long. His ambition wouldn't allow it. He would strike, thinking he had the upper hand. That, however, would not be the case!

DiGeorgio was a survivor. He had fought in a lot of wars, and he had emerged victorious. He would survive this one as well. He couldn't say the same for Fast Eddie Falcone. No, Eddie was out there in the night, singing his death song. He just didn't know that he was a dead man walking!

~ ~ ~

Luke watched the convoy leave and started making his way back to his car. He had to keep eyes on DiGeorgio if he was to have any chance of preventing the violence that he was sure would erupt on the San Diego streets.

He was halfway down the hill when he spotted somebody making their way up the hill. Luke Santos froze, crouching down as he stepped off the trail and waited. Was this one of DiGeorgio's people making a routine patrol? Or was it something else? The only way to find out was to wait for the guy to reach him and take him down. Luke had his pistol in his fist, ready to fire if need be. The shadow moved closer, accompanied by a lot of wheezing breathes as if he was out of shape. "Jake?" Luke asked from the darkness.

"Luke?"

"I thought you wanted no part of this."

"I let my pride get the better of me. I couldn't let you come out here alone."

"Let's head for your car. DiGeorgio just left and I don't want to lose him," Luke said.

"Swell," Arnold groaned as he turned and headed down the hill, gasping all the way.

~ ~ ~

"Those two cops are major fuck-ups," Gabriel King shook his head.

"Why? Because they came to do their jobs despite having their asses chewed for the earlier fiasco?" Phillips asked.

"No, because they should have left this case to us."

"Did you know that DiGeorgio had just left?"

"That's beside the point."

"No, King, it is not."

"Po-ta-toe, po-tat-o," King growled.

"Bullshit, King. These boys are going to lead us to Fast Eddie. Something you haven't been able to manage for most of the past year," Phillips told him.

"You're right about that, Renee."

"I know I am."

"I figured that out all ready," King sighed.

Chapter Nineteen

Cooper and the others got to Oceanside Pier early. Cooper wanted to scout the place out before DiGeorgio and company arrived. "Where do you want me?" Rico asked.

"Find a spot close to the parking area. As much as I'd love to take these two out onto the pier to make the exchange, there is too big a risk that innocent people would get hurt. No, we'll have to do it here in the parking area, but maybe close to the amphitheater," Cooper replied.

"What if there is a show going on?"

"Then we set up at the opposite end of the parking lot, as far away from crowds as possible. I don't want any innocents hurt."

"I get that. I just wanted to be sure," Rico said.

"You starting to have doubts?" Cooper asked.

"Not really, no. I just want to make sure we are on the same page."

"I respect and understand that, Enrico. I think we'll work well together."

"I hope so, Mitch," Rico said.

~ ~ ~

Leo was driving, a fact that Julian DiGeorgio drew comfort from. Leo had been with him from the beginning. Nobody in his "family" was more loyal than Leo. Julian trusted him over Arty and Benji both. That was why Leo was his number one wheelman and his number one body guard.

Julian had no doubt that Leo would be willing to die for him if need be!

"We're about five minutes out, Boss," Leo said.

"Check your weapons boys. I want you on high alert just in case this isn't on the up and up," DiGeorgio told his men. Benji spread the word to the other two vehicles via radio.

~ ~ ~

Fast Eddie had watched the convoy leave the house and he was running a loose track on them, following to see where they were headed. He was surprised that Calabresi had stayed behind, and that DiGeorgio had let him. He shook his head. Would wonders never cease?

Getting DiGeorgio away from Calabresi might well work in his favor. Especially if DiGeorgio didn't come back and Fast Eddie showed up in his place. Eddie Falcone smiled at the thought. He liked the idea. Sure, Calabresi wouldn't exactly welcome him with open arms, but he could understand that. But Calabresi was a business man. He knew that a vacuum would mean trouble. If Eddie was ready to step in to fill that vacuum, then it would be a smoother transition. One thing that Eddie was sure of. Julian DiGeorgio was going to die tonight!

~ ~ ~

Luke Santos was driving as he trailed along behind the DiGeorgio caravan. There were a few cars ahead of him, but he was okay with that. It would make him and Arnold harder to spot. "Why did you come, Jake? You made it clear that you wanted to back away and let the chips fall where they may," Luke asked.

"You think maybe I came because I felt ashamed of the way I acted? That I felt bad about abandoning my partner when I knew he was heading into a dangerous situation?" Jake Arnold asked.

"I can believe it, but I'm not sure anyone else would," Luke told him.

"They don't matter to me. You do. I wasn't always a lazy ass cop, Kid. You made me see that the job was still worth doing. I hadn't felt that way for a long time," Jake replied.

"I'm glad to hear that. You have any idea where these guys might be going?"

"I wish I knew," Jake Arnold replied.

~ ~ ~

"I think we might be headed to Oceanside Pier," Renee Phillips said as Gabriel King guided their unmarked Dodge Charger through the streets of San Diego.

"Why is that?" Gabriel King asked.

"The direction we are headed for one thing. Plus, if Cooper has something to trade for his client's life, he would want to do it somewhere public, but also in a place where he could make sure that innocent civilians wouldn't be hurt. Oceanside Pier fits all of the criteria," Renee Phillips shrugged.

"That actually makes sense," King nodded.

"That almost sounded like a compliment."

"Maybe because it was one?"

"Will wonders never cease?"

"Can you stop busting my chops, even for a minute?" King asked her in exasperation.

"I can, but where would be the fun in that?" she asked, smiling.

"I'm not sure, but I think we might find a middle ground."

"Middle ground would be good."

"I thought so too."

~ ~ ~

Mike Gordon frowned as Mitch Cooper pulled into a parking space. He was thankful that Giselle had remained quiet, though he was sure that had more to do with the duct tape over her mouth. Fast Eddie would shoot him as quickly as looking at him once he found out that they had failed in their mission. Poor Giselle had no idea what fate had in store for her.

She was dead and didn't even know it. Gordon closed his eyes. He hated that. From what he had gotten to know about her, Giselle wasn't really a bad kid. She had just made some really bad choices in life. He hadn't helped. If she died, it would be on him.

This was his entire fault. He should never have dragged her into it. An innocent young woman was going to die because of him, and there really wasn't a damn thing that he could do about it. Cooper got out and opened the door and helped him out of the car. The man held a wicked looking gun on him, and the hammer was back. The private eye obviously wasn't taking any chances.

The kid got Giselle out of the car, and once Cooper had them both under his gun, the kid disappeared in the parking lot. Cooper had them lean on the back of the rental while he covered them with the gun. There was some kind of concert going on and they could hear the music. Gordon sighed as he waited for his end to come.

~ ~ ~

Rico Verdes crouched down a row over and four cars down, the sling of the Mossberg tight over his shoulder. He kept the tension on the sling, keeping the weapon ready to fire. He had already jacked a round into the chamber and added another round to the tubular magazine. His heart was beating rapidly, but his breathing was regular. He felt like he had in the service, just before a firefight.

His vision was in hyper-focus, everything seemed clearer and bigger as the adrenaline shot through his system. His body was a picture of constrained tension. He was a taut string of a bow, aching to be released and send the arrow flying towards its target.

~ ~ ~

Mitch Cooper leaned easily on the car next to the rental that Gordon had provided. On the outside, he was the picture of calm. On the inside, he was twitching like a meth tweaker ready for a fix. Adrenaline was flooding his bloodstream while he waited for Julian DiGeorgio to arrive. That was the bad part about setting up a meet like this. You were at the mercy of the other party as far as knowing when they would arrive.

Anything could delay them. Traffic, a wreck on the highway, a traffic stop. It couldn't be predicted. Murphy's Law was a factor in any mission, and Mr. Murphy was one fickle son of a bitch. Cooper had learned that back in his SEAL days. Then he spotted the convoy pulling off the highway into the parking lot. Cooper breathed a sigh of relief, feeling some of the tension drain away.

Sure, he could still get killed, but at least DiGeorgio had shown, which meant that there was a good chance that he would be able to get Rico off the hook with this trade. Cooper walked over to the pair and slipped two small two-shot derringers into their pockets. Their survival would now be up to them. Cooper stepped away and into the headlights of the approaching cars.

"You the guy that called?" asked a familiar voice.

"I am," Cooper replied. He could feel himself calming. This was something he could face. This was a known quantity.

"Which one is the cop?"

"The man. The girl is with him. The deal still good? The two of them for the kid?"

"It is. Two of my boys are going to come and take them. I'd like to ask you to back up a few feet."

"I can do that," Cooper called back. He moved back about ten yards. He kept his gun ready to swing up and start shooting if need be.

Two men emerged from the lead car and came forward. They grabbed Gordon and Giselle and marched them back to the car. Cooper watched until they were inside. "I have your word that the kid is out of this?" Cooper asked.

"As far as I am concerned, he is. Calabresi agreed. I'll make sure that DeGrassi leaves him alone as well," DiGeorgio called back.

"Then our business is concluded," Cooper said, stepping between two cars. The convoy drove past him and headed back out towards the freeway.

"That was intense," Rico said as he walked up beside Cooper.

"That it was. DiGeorgio and DeGrassi are both off your ass now. So is Calabresi. What are you going to do?"

"I guess I'm going into business with you. Will Paloma be okay?" Rico asked.

"Paloma is a survivor. I'm sure she will be fine. Why

don't you give her a call?" Cooper asked.

"I should do that," Rico agreed as he pulled out his cell phone.

~ ~ ~

"Rico?" Paloma asked, her heart beating fast. She worried about her little brother. He was her world.

"Yes, Paloma, who else would it be?" Rico asked, rolling his eyes.

"Are you safe?" she asked.

"Our friend Mitch saved me."

"Thank God."

"Paloma, you are on your own with Mr. DiGeorgio. I am free and that is what matters. Mr. Cooper has asked me to work for him, and I have accepted his offer."

"Rico," she started.

"It is not your choice to make, Paloma. It is mine. I did you the courtesy of letting you know. I am not a little boy. I am a man, and the choices that I make are my own. Nobody, especially you, will make them for me.

"I guess I understand, Enrico. I do not like it, but I understand. It is time for you to follow your own path in the world."

"Yes, it is, sister. So, I hope you will leave me to it," Rico said.

~ ~ ~

Fast Eddie had witnessed the exchange. As much as he wanted to take out Cooper, now was not the time. Not while DiGeorgio had Mike Gordon in his hands. The girl, Giselle, he could care less about. But he could not allow DiGeorgio to question Mike Gordon. Gordon knew too much about him!

Fast Eddie stepped on the gas, closing the distance. Time was of the essence, and he needed to take DiGeorgio out. Killing Gordon would be a bonus!

~ ~ ~

"Did you see that?" Luke Santos asked as he followed the four cars in front of him.

"I saw it. The car in front of us is following DiGeorgio's crew," Jake Arnold admitted.

"I think that might be the guy that shot DiGeorgio's place up this afternoon," Luke said.

"Are you sure of that?"

"Yeah, the car is the same model."

"Interesting. This actually might be a full-fledged gang war."

"Yeah, it might. So, what the hell are we going to do about it, Jake?"

"I guess we are going to stop it," Arnold replied.

"Good to know, Jake. I'm going to ram that trail car."

"Are you sure you want to do that?" Jake Arnold asked.

"Yep. You bet your ass I do," Luke replied as he stepped on the gas. He swung out like he was going to pass, and then he swung in and clipped the back of the vehicle, sending it into a spin off the side of the road. The rest of the convoy kept moving. Luke swung in behind the tail car and was out almost before he had even stopped.

Chapter Twenty

Luke slammed on the breaks and was out of the car before the other car stopped its spin, striking a telephone pole. He drew his weapon and leveled it at the man slumped over the wheel. So far, the guy hadn't moved. Santos moved closer to the car as Jake Arnold called for backup and then exited their car as well.

Luke's heart was hammering in his chest as he approached the wrecked car. This was the guy that had attacked DiGeorgio's place earlier. Luke had gotten a good look at him before he had shot up their other car earlier. He could feel his palm sweating against the grip of his pistol. The door of the car opened and the man turned towards him.

"Freeze!" Luke yelled. He saw a flash and something slammed hard into his chest driving him backwards. He lost his grip on his pistol and it flew out of his hand as he fell back. He thought he heard Jake Arnold yell before everything went black.

~ ~ ~

Jake Arnold screamed in horror as he heard the shot and saw his partner go down. His pistol raised, almost as if of its own volition as before he even realized it, he was firing. The man in the car twisted and turned as bullets hammered into him before falling on the ground, blood flowering on his shirt from multiple wounds.

Arnold moved forward, keeping his pistol on the man.

He kicked the man's gun away before running to his partner. Luke groaned and pushed to a sitting position. "That hurt," he rasped.

"Getting shot does, even when you're wearing a vest," Jake told him, breathing a sigh of relief. The kid had worn his vest. He was learning.

"Did we get the guy?" Luke asked.

"We got him," Jake replied. He went back to the car and called in the officer down and for a bus. The kid would probably complain about it, but Arnold wanted him checked out by the EMT's. He called for the coroner's wagon as well for the dead man.

~ ~ ~

"So what do we do now?" Rico asked Cooper.

"What do you mean?" Cooper looked at him.

"We can't let DiGeorgio kill those two."

"No, we can't. But we did agree to exchange them for you. So, what do you suggest?" Cooper asked.

"I could care less about Gordon. He was a crooked cop, so he deserves whatever happens to him. Giselle didn't know what she was getting herself in to. Fast Eddie and Gordon both lied to her," Rico sighed.

"I agree. So what do you want to do about it?" Cooper asked.

"I don't know. I was hoping that you might have a suggestion."

"I might, but it would mean you might have to make a deal with your sister."

"I can do that," Rico nodded.

~ ~ ~

"They are heading back to DiGeorgio's house," Renee

Phillips said.

"So, it appears. How do you think those cops faired with that other car?" King asked.

"Hard to say, but I think they probably got the bad guy they were after."

"Which leaves these guys for us."

"Yes, it does."

~ ~ ~

Julian DiGeorgio looked at the dirty cop. He didn't care about the girl. She was superfluous. But the cop. He belonged to Fast Eddie. He would know things.

DiGeorgio frowned. How much did Calabresi know? Could he have set this whole thing in process? It was something to think about. His phone chirped. He picked it up an answered. "Hello?"

"Mister DiGeorgio. This is Mitch Cooper. I'm the guy that made the deal with you," Mitch Cooper told him.

"So why are you calling me, Cooper?" DiGeorgio asked.

"I want the girl. She had nothing to do with this. She was pulled into it by the cop."

"Why should I care?"

"Because deep down, I think you might be a good man. Gordon is the one that was working directly for Falcone. He set the girl up and forced her to set the kid up. She's just another victim. Let her go, and word will get around about what a benevolent guy you are. Benevolence can ensure better loyalty than fear," Cooper explained.

"I'm listening. What exactly are you suggesting?" DiGeorgio asked.

"Despite what she did to him, the kid has a soft spot for the girl. He doesn't want to see her harmed. Would you be willing to let his sister take the girl back up to San Clemente?"

"I think that can be arranged."

"Then we have a deal?"

"Yes. But Cooper?"

"Yes?"

"I never want to hear from you again," DiGeorgio told him.

"That's a promise that I can't make, Sir. Given my profession. I will, however always approach you with respect," Cooper told him.

"I can accept that," DiGeorgio replied, hanging up his cell phone. He looked at Mike Gordon and the cop's face went pale. "Tell me about Fast Eddie Falcone and everything you've done for him."

~ ~ ~

"Looks like they are heading back to DiGeorgio's place," Phillips said.

"I wonder what they want with the two that they picked up." Gabriel King muttered. "And why did Cooper hand them over? What the hell is going on here?"

"That's the question isn't it, Agent King?" Renee Phillips looked over at him.

"I know Cooper is involved up to his ears in this," King spat.

"You don't even know what this is. Why is that so hard for you to admit? Is it because you're a man?

"You're right, Phillips. I don't know what we have stumbled into. However, I do intend to find out."

"I've no doubt of that. Even when you're wrong, you're never uncertain."

"Bite me, Renee."

"Not going to happen, Gabriel. I don't know where you've been," Phillips replied, grinning.

~ ~ ~

Paloma Verdes paced the floor. She was glad to know that Rico was safe from harm. She was less than pleased about his decision to start working with the private investigator, but there was nothing she could do about that.

She sighed. Deep down, she knew that she was really the one that had gotten Enrico into trouble to begin with. She had talked Julian into sending that package on Rico's truck. Perhaps it was time that she stopped trying to mother him and let grow up. She had no doubt that he would make her proud one day.

~ ~ ~

Leo pulled the car into the driveway. He was relieved that things had gone so smooth. Despite his loyalty to his boss, Leo knew that he was getting too old to get into shooting wars. He turned off the ignition and scrambled around to get DiGeorgio's door. He opened it and stood waiting as his boss climbed out. Once the two prisoners were out, the party moved inside.

~ ~ ~

"Now who do you suppose those two were?" King asked from down the block where he and Phillips had parked.

"I don't know, but they sure looked like they were in trouble," Renee replied.

"Yes, they did, and I don't think our badges are going to impress a Mafia kingpin like Julian DiGeorgio," King said.

"For once I agree with you."

"Will wonders never cease? How about you call your

buddies on the police force and tell them what we saw? I'm sure they have a SWAT team that's sitting around eating donuts."

"Based on that remark I should let you walk in there by yourself. However, I'm not a person to hold grudges. I'll make the call," Phillips said.

~ ~ ~

Giselle was frightened. She had gotten over being mad quite a bit earlier. Who were these men? What were they going to do to her? She felt a tear start to trickle down her cheek. She didn't want to die. Then a well-dressed Hispanic woman stepped into the room. She cut the duct tape that secured Giselle's wrists behind her. Then she waited while Giselle tore the tape off of her mouth, wincing at the pain.

"I've been told to take you back to San Clemente. You are to forget any of this ever happened. If you tell anyone, especially the police, then someone will come and kill you. Tell me you understand," the woman said in a cold voice.

"I—I understand," Giselle sobbed.

"Then come with me," Paloma told her, leading her back out to her car. The two women got in and drove off.

Mike Gordon stood in front of both Julian DiGeorgio and Vincent Calabresi, looking from one to the other. He knew he would probably die. "I want you to tell Mr. Calabresi here what you told me about Eddie Falcone. Then we will decide if you get to live or not."

Mike Gordon started talking. Thirty minutes later, he was walking out the door under his own power. He wasn't sure who was more surprised, him or the half dozen cops that were coming up the steps with guns drawn.

~ ~ ~

Mitch Cooper stood on the beach, listening to the sound of the surf. The sun felt good on his face. He felt at peace, at least for the moment. It wouldn't last. He understood that. He liked the kid, Enrico. He was glad that he had been able to get him out from under the mob. Cooper took a deep breath and then blew it out slowly.

"Hey Sailor, you looking for a good time?" asked a familiar female voice from behind him. Cooper grinned as he turned.

"That depends on what you have in mind, Kara," he said. He was pleased to see the small almost pixie-like brunette he had met on a case a while back.

"I was in town and I thought we might do some more testing on your theory," Kara Quentin smiled up at him.

"Which theory was that?" Cooper asked.

"The one on Cosmic sex."

"Do you have a new theory to test?"

"I'm sure we can think of one," Cooper told her. And they did.

Thank you for reading.
Please review this book. Reviews help others find
Absolutely Amazing eBooks and inspire us to keep
providing these marvelous tales.

If you would like to be put on our email list to receive
updates on new releases, contests, and promotions, please
go to AbsolutelyAmazingEbooks.com and sign up.

Mitch Cooper Mysteries
Next in the Series

OR DIE TRYING

It starts out as a rescue mission and turns into a fight for survival! Maria Ramirez is a leading defense attorney in San Diego. But when her daughter goes missing, she turns to Private investigator Mitch Cooper to find her daughter. Maria suspects it was the girl's father that took her but Cooper isn't so sure. Estaban Quintana is the girl's father and he is a high ranking member of the *Los Noches* drug Cartel. But Cooper's investigation leads him toward Marco Iberia, a member of the *Diablo Loco* an up and coming drug gang that wants to take over *Los Noches* drug operations. To recover the girl and get her back to her mother, Cooper may have to make a deal with the devil to survive or die trying!

About the Author

Bill Craig published his first novel at age 40 and says it only took him 34 years to become an overnight success! He has been publishing steadily ever since that first book Valley of Death and now has more books published than Carter has Little Liver Pills.

ABSOLUTELY AMAZING eBOOKS

AbsolutelyAmazingEbooks.com
or AA-eBooks.com